Let's CHEAT!

GENE TAYLOR

Dreamspinner Press

Published by
Dreamspinner Press
5032 Capital Circle SW
Ste 2, PMB# 279
Tallahassee, FL 32305-7886
USA
http://www.dreamspinnerpress.com/

Let's Cheat

Cover Art by Paul Richmond
http://www.paulrichmondstudio.com

ISBN: 978-1-62380-299-8
Digital ISBN: 978-1-62380-300-1

Printed in the United States of America
First Edition
January 2013

This story is dedicated to my friend since high school and college days—Ronnie Lang—who has traveled the long road from Monterey Cantores to beta proofread! Thanks, treasured buddy!

PROLOGUE

THE attractive blond man looked anxiously through the backseat side window as the taxi drove up to a bar in a seedy section of New York City. The red-and-blue blinking neon sign that announced "Killer Joe's" made the man even more nervous. The cabbie stopped the vehicle and waited as his passenger hesitated.

"Are you sure that this is the right place?" the blond asked.

"It's the address you gave me. Now, are you in or out? The meter's still running."

"Okay, I guess I'm out," the blond said, handing cash to the driver and then opening the door. "I don't suppose you'd wait for me, just in case I got the address wrong...."

"Not on your life, buddy. I don't drive around here much, and I don't plan to risk my life by staying a minute after you get outta the cab."

The cabbie was true to his word as he sped off down the street the second that the blond man slammed the door shut.

As he stood on the sidewalk, the man looked around apprehensively, shrugged his shoulders, and cautiously walked up to the entrance. "It's now or never, I guess," he muttered as he pushed the door open and walked inside.

Loud electric noise, hardly music, hit him in the face, but the blond looked left and right and then straight ahead before he slowly, almost stumbling, made his way up to the bar. "What do you have on tap?" he asked the bartender.

"Beer," replied the bartender, one of the ugliest men he had ever seen.

The missing front tooth and the barbed wire earrings made the blond shiver slightly. Sharp laughter rang out around him as he turned red. He was already regretting that he had agreed to come to this fearsome place. This was like a zoo with human animals who wore glittering piercings, black leather, and tight white T-shirts stretched over heavily pumped muscles. They all looked like they really belonged behind bars too. Prison bars.

"Okay, beer, then," the blond mumbled as he fished a bill from his wallet, and then he carefully returned the wallet to an inside, hopefully secure pocket.

The bartender grinned, proudly displaying that black gap. He slid the glass of beer along the slick bar to the blond and watched. Several patrons around the blond had now turned to stare at this awkward-acting newcomer who certainly didn't look as if he belonged here. This preppy, youngish man wearing a plaid shirt and a backpack looked more than a little suspicious to the assorted rough types now eying him. He was beginning to feel a lot like Bambi in headlights.

He picked up his beer and turned around, frantically searching for someone. From in the distance, through layers of cigarette smoke near the back of the bar he heard a voice calling. "Over here," it said. "Come on over here!"

At just that moment he felt a hand reach out to grab his ass. The hand began to rub in circles around first one cheek and then the other. Suddenly someone else's hand found his crotch and started to explore and massage, gently at first and then harder. Panicked, the blond man almost dropped his beer and whirled away from the probing hands as he tried to navigate toward the voice he'd heard. Again there was that crude laughter as he fled to the back of the bar.

"Would you get over here and stop fooling around!" the voice commanded as the blond man approached a table near the back wall of the bar.

"How come you picked such a dangerous, crummy place like this to meet?" the blond exploded in a loud whisper as he sank into a chair next to an equally attractive dark-haired young man.

"Never mind all that," the man replied. "Did you bring it?"

"*Oh, darn*, I forgot," the blond said sarcastically. "Of course, you *dummy*. Why else would I be wearing this backpack like some naïve college-boy tourist?" He reached to one shoulder and then the other as he took off the backpack and laid it on the table.

"Not here in front of everybody!" the dark-haired man protested.

"Oh yeah. Like anybody but you could see it in this dark pit of hell. Have you got your part?"

"Of course I do. Just let me have a quick look inside this backpack." He unzipped the top and checked the plastic bags of white powder all lined up in rows. He smiled, apparently satisfied. "Okay, here you go." He reached under his chair and brought out a small black briefcase. "Check it out."

The blond unsnapped the top of the briefcase and glanced inside at the neat stacks of twenty-dollar bills in bundles. He closed it back up and began to slide the case off the table.

That was when the world exploded. Four of the meanest-looking thugs possible suddenly appeared and effectively surrounded the table, blocking the view from the other bar patrons.

"Looky what we got here," said the one who seemed to be the leader. "These two nice college girls have brought refreshments to the party." He flashed a wicked-looking knife. "We'll just relieve you of the goodies, and thanks for the cash too."

One of the men took the briefcase, and another took the backpack.

"What do you want to do with *these ladies*?" asked the fourth.

The leader examined his knife as though he hadn't seen it before. "Does this look like a good carving knife to you guys?" He grinned at the shaking men.

The blond man turned to the dark-haired man and squealed, "This is all *your* fault!"

Chapter
ONE

Several weeks earlier…

BRADLEY MOORE carefully popped his left eye open and stared straight ahead in the deepening glow of a Tuesday morning. It took a few seconds to focus, and then he opened the other eye. He needed both to decipher the red digits on the bedside alarm clock because he hadn't yet put in his contact lenses. It was a blurry 6:26—four minutes before the alarm would scream out that awful but necessary morning buzz. Bradley always felt a sense of accomplishment if he could wake up before his electric taskmaster forced him. He would have turned off the alarm before it squawked, but he felt that his bed partner, Matt, deserved the honor.

With an impish grin, Bradley eased himself out of bed, fumbled through a drawer for his best green boxer underwear, and silently padded into the bathroom. He knew he only had seconds to get into the shower before the alarm sounded and Matt began to grumble and curse at the clock. Bradley chuckled as the buzz began, a split second before the water's spray drowned out the sounds of a heavy sleeper arising for the day. Bradley laughed out loud, knowing that no one, meaning Matt in the bedroom, heard him.

"DAMN it," Matt Sharp bellowed at the empty space where Bradley had lain, as well as at the offending alarm clock. "He did it again, that bastard." He stretched and swung his arm in the general direction of the squawking intrusion, taking three swats to finally hit the right button.

Once he was out of bed with the cursed alarm silenced, Matt gathered his clothes from various drawers and the big walk-in closet before dropping them onto the only chair in the room. Then he sat down grumpily at the foot of the bed to wait impatiently for his turn in the shower. He could hear his soul mate's lusty singing through the bathroom door. *The bastard's doing that on purpose to annoy me.*

But since Bradley usually got up first and gleefully left the alarm to shatter Matt's dreams, Matt knew he only had himself to blame for being a sleepyhead in the morning. *Maybe I'll set the alarm on my watch one of these days and beat him at his own game.* Matt chuckled at the thought.

The bathroom door opened and a still-damp and naked Bradley came strolling out with a huge grin on his handsome face.

"All yours, your majesty," Bradley joked. He tried to dodge when Matt made a run at him.

Instead of smacking Bradley, Matt grabbed him and planted a passionate, soulful kiss that grew in intensity as it lingered. Then Matt broke from the kiss and smiled triumphantly. "That's what you get for hogging the shower."

Bradley laughed. "That was supposed to be a punishment?"

"That was a pre-mouthwash kiss. I hope my breath was just awful."

This time Bradley just grinned. "In that case I'll tell you something. I love your kisses no matter what... and I just flooded my mouth with mint mouthwash. You may be disappointed that I didn't notice a thing. Nice try though."

Matt shrugged and glided back into Bradley's arms. "Okay. You win... and I love you anyway." He gave Bradley a quick kiss and shuffled into the bathroom, leaving Bradley to get dressed.

BY THE time Matt finally finished showering, shaving, and dressing for the day, he could smell the pungent coffee aroma drifting from the kitchen down the hall. At least there was the consolation that Bradley had had to make breakfast for them both. With a final adjustment to his tie, Matt made for the kitchen table where Bradley sat, a steaming mug in hand, flashing a self-satisfied grin at him.

"Morning, lover," Bradley said. "Sleep well?"

"Good morning, bastard," Matt replied with a mock frown that merged into a smile as he leaned over and planted another kiss on Bradley's lips, warm and tasty from the coffee. "I could have awakened a little more happily without that alarm though."

"Yeah, but then you'd oversleep and miss your first lecture. What's today's topic, Professor?"

"Associate professor," Matt corrected. "Today we're going to review notes on the Third Crusade to get my students ready for an essay quiz next week."

"Darn, but I hate to miss that. I just know how *exciting* that will be," Bradley added with only a tiny touch of sarcasm. "One of these days I'm going to surprise you and actually sit in on one of your classes. I know you really do bring all that history stuff to life, sweetie."

"Thanks. I try. But some of it isn't all that thrilling to me, either. But I love history... and you, too, of course. Not that we have *that* much history."

"Eight years next month. And no, I haven't forgotten," Bradley pointed out. "You're not the only one who remembers dates."

Matt sipped some of the coffee he had poured. "Well, at least the date is easy to remember since we can celebrate the day we met *as well as* our wedding anniversary on the same day. I think we were pretty smart to combine them like that. Lucky for us we could both get away at the same time to fly to California the way we did. I just loved getting married to you."

"You'd better have. I don't plan to ever marry anyone else."

"That makes two of us."

"Only four years ago, and it seems like ten," Bradley said with a grin.

"Okay, ball and chain, two can say that."

"Just teasing. Golly, look at the clock. I've got to grab my briefcase and get going...."

"Are you in court today or just in the office?"

Bradley grimaced. "I wish it were a case in court, but this is just another research day in our law library and on the Internet. I'm helping with a couple of cases for two of the senior partners. Anyway, Grace seems to like me since she does let me assist her in court from time to time. Not that I get to do or say as much as I'd like when I'm there at the table with her. But at least she's also started to let me handle more cases by myself lately. Uh oh." He glanced at the kitchen clock. "I have to *go*." He pulled Matt close for a real morning kiss.

Matt slowly released Bradley. "I love you, but you need another quick dose of mouthwash... unless you're advertising Dunkin' Donuts coffee."

"I love you back, and I've just got time for that quick gargle. See you tonight."

True to his word, Bradley practically ran to the bathroom, gargled, and rushed out of the apartment.

"Hope you can get a cab, Bradley," Matt said to the empty kitchen. "And there better be one for me when I get these dishes in the dishwasher." He trailed off to silence.

Grace McKenna glanced up from her desk in time to see Bradley rushing by the oversized window of her office as he hurried to his own small cubicle. She pressed the intercom button on her desk. "Marge, buzz Bradley Moore and ask him to come to my office at once, please. And thanks."

Grace watched in amusement through her window as she saw Bradley drop his briefcase on his desk and pick up his phone. With a satisfied smile, she saw that he wasted no time answering her summons.

Since she knew the knock on the door that quickly followed was Bradley, she called for him to enter. Then, hiding an amused grin at Bradley's obvious haste, she gestured to him to have a seat in front of her desk. "Good morning, Bradley," she began pleasantly as she looked approvingly at one of her favorites. "I hope you have a minute to spare," she teased.

"Hi, Grace. You know I'm always at your beck and call, so to speak," he replied with a wink.

"You're such a gentleman, Bradley. That's only one of the reasons I like you so much. How's Matt?"

Bradley seemed to relax a bit. "He's fine and in the middle of the Third Crusade, he says."

She chuckled. "I like history too. Actually it was my undergraduate minor. I hope all is well between you two."

"Oh yes. We're just fine. Both of us are busy as always, you know."

"That's why I asked you to come in to see me this morning. I know you've already been really swamped this week with background research for a couple of the senior partners, but something has come up in that Donavan case I'm working. I hate to ask you, Bradley, but I really do need some information very quickly to help me sort out some details. I'm afraid this may be a very long day for you, and will likely run a little into the evening as well, but it just can't be helped."

Bradley replied at once. "Of course, Grace. Anything for you." He smiled again. "Matt and I didn't really have any big plans for tonight anyway. Besides, it's just part of the job to take care of our clients, no matter how much extra time it takes."

"You have a really terrific attitude, Bradley—as always." She stood and offered her hand. "Rest assured that all your hard work will benefit you in the future. I can promise you that."

"Thanks, Grace. I appreciate that. And I guess I'd better get started. Do you have a list of what you need? I'll call Matt and tell him that I'll be later than I expected."

THE bell rang ending the class. "And don't forget," Matt thundered above the noise as students gathered their belongings and headed for the door, "we have a quiz next time. Study your notes, and *read those chapters.*"

Matt stepped to his desk and sat down to relax for a few minutes. This had been his last class for the day, and he was feeling somewhat exhausted from reviewing the Crusades for the second time within three hours. He looked forward to a relaxing evening at home with Bradley. *Maybe we'll have dinner out tonight and then just watch a DVD. It's been a while since Bradley and I have just had a quiet evening together. Work for both of us seems to interfere with our personal time a lot lately.*

Kristen Spears's office was next door to Matt's. The history department had thoughtfully put them close together. They had known each other for several years, ever since his first year as a novice instructor at the college, and it was rather handy to have a friendly neighbor.

"Oh, Matt! I'm so glad that you're still here."

Surprised, Matt looked up and saw his next-door colleague in the history department. "Hi there, gorgeous. What's up?"

"You've just *got* to help me out, Matt," she said. "I've got a family emergency, and I have to drive out of town for the evening. Could you cover my undergraduate Western civilization class tonight? I've brought my notes for the lecture. You could have one of the secretaries type up the notes, but maybe you could run through them briefly with the students... answering any questions if there are any. It could be a short class. Oh *please, please, please*," she begged.

Matt felt the hopes of a cozy evening with Bradley slowly fading away. "I actually was planning a special evening alone with Bradley...," he said.

"You can do that anytime, handsome. There really isn't any choice for me. I just *have* to go tonight, and my students really need these notes. I'm pleading with you now," she added. "And I promise that I'll make it up to you, whatever favor you might need sometime. Whenever you like."

His resistance gone, Matt simply nodded. "Okay, I'll do it, but you really do owe me *big time,* you realize."

Kristen dashed up to him and planted a kiss on his cheek. "Oh, thanks so much, Matt. You're an angel." She handed him a file folder with several pages of notes. "I've got to go."

She practically raced out of the classroom, and Matt stared at the clock. He had about an hour and a half to get everything prepared for this evening. Luckily, Kristen had left him the class rolls so he knew how many copies to make.

Hmmm... I better call Bradley with the bad news. He selected the speed dial option on his iPhone, but the call went straight to voice mail. "I guess that's better than texting," he said, and left the message.

BRADLEY sat at a table in his law firm's library. He glanced at the lower right hand side of his laptop and saw the time. *Uh oh. I guess I'd better call Matt and let him know I'll be late.* He dialed the number, but the phone went directly to voice mail. "Hey, Matt honey, it's me. I guess we'll have to wait a bit for a night together at home because...."

IT WAS a little after nine thirty before Matt finally got off the elevator and trudged down the hallway to his and Bradley's apartment. After his long day, his normally brisk pace had slowed down considerably. He reached his door and was just about to put his key into the lock when the door of the next apartment opened, and his good friend Clarice Tinsley came bounding out into the hall.

"Matthew," she exclaimed. "I'm so glad you're *finally* home. I've been running next door every fifteen minutes or so to see if you were here yet."

"Why didn't you just call?" Matt replied wearily as he unlocked his door. "Wouldn't that have been a lot easier?"

"I did, and when you check your voice mail for messages, you'll hear a bunch from me. Besides, you know how you sometimes forget to check."

Nodding, Matt asked, "Can I help you with something, Clarice? What's so important that you had to keep popping over here?"

"Aren't you going to ask me in? I've really wanted to talk to you...."

"I'm *so* beat. Could it wait until tomorrow?"

Her face filled with disappointment. "Really? You couldn't spare me just a few minutes? We could sit on the sofa and have a cup of cocoa. I'll go make some in my apartment and bring it over," she suggested hopefully.

Matt smiled at his best friend. "Okay, but we really have to keep it kind of short. I've had a long day, and Bradley will be exhausted when he gets home too. I guess he's not back yet, or he would have answered the door when you knocked."

"I'll be back in a flash."

"Hold it, Clarice. I've got some hot chocolate mix you can use. Just go ahead and use our kitchen. I'll change clothes and then meet you on the couch. I'll be trying to keep my eyes open."

She beamed with pleasure. "Fine. Did I tell you that you're my favorite gay boy?"

"I'll bet you tell Bradley the same thing," Matt replied as he ushered Clarice into the apartment. "Let me get changed and check my voice mail—then I'll be back." He grinned. "And no sneaking into the bedroom while I'm not looking so you can watch me undress."

She laughed. "You're cute, but I know a lost cause when I see one. You're already taken by that gorgeous dreamboat that lives with you. Don't take too long," she cautioned. "I have to go home and get some beauty sleep too, you know."

Considering how fatigued he felt, Matt emerged fairly quickly to find Clarice waiting with two mugs of steaming cocoa on the coffee table, each one crowned on top with whipped cream.

"Bradley left me a message, and he had to work late too."

"I found the can of Reddi-wip in the fridge," she explained as she saw his smile. "You look really sexy in those shorts. And I love your teddy bear T-shirt."

"That was a gift from Bradley. He thinks it's cute so I wear it to please him."

She handed him his cup. "So how is *Bratt*?" she asked as she settled her ample frame into a cozy corner of the sofa with her favorite cushion behind her.

Matt recoiled from the heat of the cup. "This is still a little too hot." He set it back on the coaster on the table. "And what do you mean? Who is Bratt?"

Clarice smiled. "Didn't I tell you? It's a nickname I call you two behind your backs. I think it's fun. I got the idea from *As the World Turns* before it got cancelled. The fans used to combine the names of their favorite couples on the show. There was Carly and Jack who were Carjack. And there was Meg and Paul who became Peg. And my favorite was the one for Luke and Noah. The fans called them Nuke."

"Okay, okay. I get the idea. I don't have time to watch soaps so I didn't know what you were talking about."

"Well, you see how it works... so naturally Bradley and Matt are... *Bratt*," she proudly exclaimed with a big grin.

"I'm surprised that you don't call us *Madley*," he said with a crooked smile.

She laughed. "I thought about it, and it almost fits as well. But I like *Bratt* better—it fits your personalities. Now to get back to my original question. How *is* Bratt?"

"Bratt is fine, I guess. We just don't see each other all that much anymore."

"Do I detect trouble in paradise?"

Matt frowned. "Not exactly trouble. We've just gotten so busy with our careers that sometimes I feel that we're more like roommates than a married couple. It makes me sad to say it."

"Are you saying that your jobs are keeping you both too busy to have a good marriage anymore?"

"No, our marriage isn't in trouble. It's true that we're really busy a lot of the time, but there's more to it than just that. We do the *same things* all the time, we go to the *same places*, we're kind of in a boring routine a lot of the time. Our life together isn't that much *fun* anymore like it used to be. That's the real problem. We've become boring and need to spice things up between us."

"I kind of had a feeling you might say something like that," she said, shaking her auburn curls. "That's why I was thinking about you two today while I was watching television."

"You weren't at work?"

"I didn't go in until after lunch today. The head librarian said I could have a half day off. I guess it was sort of like compensation time for my working late a few times last week. But you got me off track."

"Heaven forbid I should get you off the subject, whatever it is," Matt said with a sly smile.

Clarice gave him a mock frown. "Anyway, I was watching the *Today* show this morning, and they had this author of a new book on there. I forget the exact title, although I'm going to look it up tomorrow. It had something to do with cheating—"

At that moment the front door opened, and Bradley practically staggered into the room. "Hey, everybody," he yawned, putting a hand over his mouth.

Matt immediately stood up and went to Bradley. He gave him a quick kiss and a welcoming hug. "Oh, sweetheart, you really do look bushed. Are you okay?"

Bradley rested his chin on Matt's shoulder and snuggled into his arms. "I'm all right, but you aren't wrong. These late hours of doing research really take it out of me. I can barely stand."

Taking the hint, Clarice stood and took the two cups to the kitchen.

Matt still stood cuddled in Bradley's arm, and he could hear Clarice rinsing cups and putting them into the dishwasher. "Hear that? She's such a good friend."

"I'm on my way home," she vowed when she came back from the kitchen. "You two get a good night's rest."

She paused only long enough to plant a quick kiss on each man's cheek.

"Good to see you, Clarice," Matt said. "Laters—"

"Hope to visit with you sometime, Clarice, when I finally stop being so busy," Bradley said sleepily.

"Good night," she replied, closing the door firmly behind her.

"She's here kind of late," Bradley said. "Is anything wrong?"

Matt smiled. "I really don't know what she wanted. It was something to do with some TV show she was watching earlier. It doesn't matter. Let's get you ready for bed. I think we both need some rest."

"Absolutely," Bradley agreed as he headed for the bedroom as Matt turned off all the living room and kitchen lights.

Moments later Bradley and Matt were cuddled together in bed, already fast asleep.

Chapter
TWO

FRIDAY afternoon couldn't have come soon enough for Matt. As soon as he got home after his last class for the week, he changed into shorts and a T-shirt and waited for Bradley to get home from the law offices. The chilled bottle of water he sipped tasted like some kind of golden elixir after his hectic week. At just that moment, his iPhone sounded out the special ringtone he'd set for Clarice.

"Don't answer this call," the phone blared in its heavy gangster-sounding prerecorded voice. "This is somebody you don't want to talk to, so don't even look at the phone 'cause it's one of those numbers you don't even want to answer! Don't answer this call!"

Matt chuckled as he always did when he heard the funny message he'd assigned as Clarice's ringtone. He picked up the phone and pressed a button. "Hi. What's up?"

"I wondered if I could come over for just a few minutes. I know it's Friday and that you and Bradley probably have plans for tonight, but I just wanted to chat for a little while. I've hardly seen you all week."

"Okay. But we really don't have a lot of time. You're right. Bradley and I do have plans tonight, and he'll be home soon. He promised."

"I'll be right over, and I truly guarantee that I won't stay long." She hung up, and her knock on the door followed in less than a minute.

"Come on in, Clarice." Matt welcomed her as he opened the door. "Want some soda or bottled water or anything?"

"No thanks. I just had a glass of iced tea when I got home a little while ago."

"So what did you want to chat about?" Matt asked. He gestured for her to join him on the sofa. "Still got something on your mind from the other day?"

"You remembered. We *did* get interrupted the other night when Bradley got home all tuckered out like that. It was something I saw on TV that I wanted to tell you about."

Matt grinned. "So what on earth did you see on the *Today* show that you've kept bottled up all week? It must be something gossipy or scandalous."

"Not at all, silly," she protested. "It was something about a book that some woman wrote. The subject was cheating on your husband."

"What? *Cheating on your husband?*" Matt's surprise turned to laughter. "That's pretty funny. Why in the world would you think that would interest me?"

"You didn't let me finish. The author was suggesting that you cheat *on* your husband... *with* your husband," Clarice said with a smile.

"Huh?"

"She was saying that when a marriage gets *boring* or *routine* or *dull*, you can spice it up by *pretending* to cheat. But you do it *with your husband.*"

Matt was intrigued. "Really? That sounds pretty far out. Tell me more about this crazy idea. Did the author give some examples of how to do this *cheating?*"

"Well," Clarice continued, "suppose you and your husband just do the same things all the time, and it's really not interesting for either of you anymore. After a while, that can be a real problem. The author was saying that you could change things up and add a little adventure to your life by role-playing. Let's say you and Bradley want to try it so you make a date to meet someplace. But you go separately and act like you don't know each other when you get there. Pretend that you're cheating by meeting someone new, but it's really just Bradley."

"But we already know each other really well. How does that help?" Matt asked.

"You're still not getting it. You *assume the identity of somebody else.* Use a different name. Make up a whole different life to tell each other—fiction of course. You can let your imagination go wild. Act like it's a secret date and just play it out, maybe even by going to a hotel together or someplace exotic that would add to the game. Do you get it now?"

Matt puzzled over all of this for a moment. "Wow. That's a really bizarre idea. And that's supposed to improve your marriage?"

"The idea is to add adventure and thrills and excitement without really cheating. The fun part is making up the scenario and acting it out. She said you could start out very simply and then make it more elaborate as you go along."

"You mean like not telling Bradley all the details of who you're going to be or what you're going to do or say?"

"That's it exactly. Doesn't that sound like a really *fun* idea? You said the other day that you and Bradley were almost not like a couple these days because you've been so busy. If you make a point to plan one of these 'cheating' dates, you might find yourselves together more than ever."

"Hmmm. It sounds good, but we're already so busy. How do we find time to do things like this?"

"I think you're missing part of the point, Matt. You have to *make time* to be together. Find a way to drop some of the more unimportant stuff in your routine to concentrate on improving your time *together*. And you don't have to do it every week or anything like that."

"I admit that I kind of like the whole crazy concept, but I'm not sure we're quite ready for something that off-the-wall. Besides, I don't know if Bradley would go along with such a thing. But I'll tell you this—I'll give it some thought. If I decide I want to try something like this, or that our marriage needs a lift like that, I'll see what Bradley has to say about it."

Clarice sighed. "If I were in a relationship that was getting away from me, I know I'd try it."

"As I said, Clarice, I'm going to give it some thought. And we'll talk about it some more later," Matt promised.

"Well, I promised I wouldn't stay very long—I'd better be on my way since I don't want to keep you from the other half of *Bratt*."

Matt groaned. "Okay. I'll see you this weekend. Maybe tomorrow the three of us might do something in the afternoon. I'll give you a call."

"Bye," Clarice called as she zipped out the door. Matt heard her own apartment door bang shut in the distance, and he sat on the sofa thoughtfully, finishing his bottle of water.

"Role-playing," he muttered.

BRADLEY finished his shower, toweled off quickly, threw on a pair of shorts, and joined Matt who was waiting on the sofa with a bottled water all ready for him.

"Better?" Matt asked.

"Much," Bradley replied, taking a long slug of his drink.

Matt leaned over and kissed Bradley before snuggling up against him. "What would you like to do tonight... besides a tumble in our bed, that is?" he asked with a grin.

Bradley kissed him back. "I guess dinner and a movie. Like we usually do on the weekend."

"Okay," Matt said. "Where shall we eat?"

"Well, we both like Domenico's in Midtown. But I doubt we could get in without a reservation on a Friday night."

"Surprise," Matt chirped. "I guess we *do* know each other pretty well. I knew you liked Domenico's so a few weeks ago I made a reservation for us for tonight."

Bradley frowned. "What if I had had to work and couldn't have made it?"

"Then Clarice and I would have had a lovely dinner," Matt replied with a sly smirk.

"You wouldn't," Bradley gasped.

"Of course I would. You don't just ignore a reservation at Domenico's. Besides, you would have done the same thing if I'd been tied up, so to speak."

"I guess," Bradley grumbled. "Anyway, that's settled. What movie do you want to see?"

"Hang on... I'm checking the multiplex listings on my iPhone. Hmmm. Want to see a romantic comedy or something else?"

"That's so *gay*. Romantic comedies, I mean. Just read off some of the titles," Bradley suggested. "I'm not up to date much on current movies these days."

"Okay, butch. Here's one for you... *The Man in the Iron Jockstrap.*"

"What? You're making that up."

Matt giggled. "I know. How about *War of the Warlocks*? Or there's *Hell in Iraq*. How about *Teen Zombie*? Anything sound good yet?"

"Are you sure these are real movies?" Bradley asked. "I must be more out of the loop than I thought."

Matt scrolled down the screen of his phone. "Let's try some of the more 'gay-sounding' titles, then. Here's one called *Love on the Run*. Or how about *Hawaiian Honeymoon*? There's one that sounds a little kinky called *Circus of Whores*. It's a double feature with *Strap It to Me, Baby*. Hmmm. Maybe that's a porn theater. Wait, this one's even better. *Nursing Home Sweethearts.*"

Bradley laughed. "Now I *know* you made that one up. You pick. This is making my head swim."

"Then let's go see *Love on the Run*. The theater isn't far from the restaurant, and it sounds like it might be fun. Come to think of it, it sounds like *our* love story these days."

"Let's change clothes, then," Bradley replied. "Domenico's is a pretty formal place. I hope my best suit isn't too wrinkled...."

DOMENICO'S maître d' seemed to have a permanently frozen smile in place above his starched white shirt and tuxedo as Bradley and Matt stepped up to his podium and gave the name for their reservation. He looked down his list.

"We're running just a little late this evening, sirs," he announced. "Would you like to wait at the bar until your table is ready? It should only be about ten minutes."

"That'll be fine," Bradley replied and followed Matt who walked ahead quickly to the only two empty spaces at the crowded bar.

"What can I get for you gentlemen?" asked a smiling, handsome young bartender.

Before Matt could even open his mouth, Bradley answered, "I'll have a scotch on the rocks, and my husband here will have a scotch sour straight-up, with an extra cherry."

"Very good, sir." The bartender faded to the back of the bar to mix the drinks.

"You didn't give me a chance to order," Matt complained.

"Huh? You always order the same thing, and so do I. What's the problem?"

Matt frowned. "That's true, I guess. But what if I had wanted something different?"

"Did you?" Bradley asked, looking a little puzzled.

"No, I guess not. But it's beginning to look like we're kind of in a rut."

The drinks arrived and Bradley took a sip of his. "You can always tell a superior restaurant by the quality of the liquor, I always say."

"You do, come to think of it. Always say that, I mean," Matt amended. He took a sip of his own drink. "But this is a little too tart, I think."

"Send it back, then," Bradley suggested.

"No. It's okay. I'll just drink it. Oh, look. Here comes the maître d'. I guess our table's ready."

"Right this way, gentlemen."

"Oh, goody!" Matt giggled after they were seated, and the maître d' had retreated. "We've got a really great window table. Look at that view."

"It just looks like New York to me," Bradley replied, glancing at the city lights.

"You're such a romantic," Matt grumbled.

After a brief apology for the wait, their server asked, "Can I get you an antipasti or insalate while you study the menu?"

Without hesitation, Bradley said, "I'll have the giant tiger shrimp cocktail, and my husband will have funghi arrostiti misti. That's pretty fancy for just pan-fried mushrooms and garlic." Bradley grinned. "And I think we're ready to order our pastas too. I'll have tortelloni al pomodoro, and he'll have the linguine alle vongole. Did you want a salad, sweetheart?"

Matt shook his head and handed his menu to the waiter. When he had left, Matt sat for a minute in silence. "Did you hear what just happened? Again."

"What do you mean?" Bradley asked innocently.

"You did it again. You just automatically ordered for me, just like with the drink."

"But isn't that what you wanted? You always order the linguine when we come here."

Matt frowned more deeply this time. "Don't you think it's a little odd that we know each other so well that you can order for me without even asking what I want? We're *terribly* predictable, Bradley."

Bradley stared at Matt. "I'll call the waiter back so you can order something else," he offered.

"No," Matt objected. "That's not the point. We're in a *rut*, we're *dull*, and we're *boring*."

Bradley tilted his head, narrowed his eyes, and said, "What? You seem to be saying stuff like that a lot lately. Are you getting tired of me, Matt?" Now he looked a little worried.

Immediately Matt reached across the table and took Bradley's hands into his own. "Absolutely *not*, sweetheart. You know how much I love you. Maybe I should just shut up about all of this, but what I meant to say was that we don't do a lot together anymore, and what we do is the same thing over and over. I was just hoping we could get a little variety into our lives. That's all."

"Oh," Bradley said, taking a deep breath. "You had me concerned about *us*."

"We're just fine, really," Matt began, only to be interrupted by the arrival of the antipasti, which effectively interrupted the discussion.

The leisurely dining completed and the short cab ride to the theater complex over, Matt and Bradley soon found themselves sitting about halfway down the theater auditorium and slightly to the left of center facing the screen. The interminable advertisements were in progress, and the coming attractions would soon follow.

"This is almost worse than TV commercials at home," Bradley whispered to Matt.

Matt nodded. "But at home you can put the TV on mute and not have to listen to all of this garbage. Well, maybe the previews will be good."

"Maybe," Bradley agreed. "So who's in this movie, anyway? I forgot to ask you."

"It's a Sandra Bullock film. I forget who the co-star is." Matt turned to Bradley. "Are you sure that you're up for this? You look awfully sleepy."

"I'm fine. Don't worry about me." But then Bradley stifled a yawn by covering his mouth. "Oh, here we go. The previews are starting."

Two or three of the coming attractions looked promising to Matt, but Bradley said nothing. Then the picture started, and Matt was instantly involved in the goofy plot as it unwound in seriously outlandish ways.

About halfway through the movie, Matt turned to Bradley and whispered, "Do you believe this ridiculous stuff?"

"I guess not," Matt answered himself softly as he glanced at Bradley and then left him sleeping undisturbed for the rest of the movie. "Oh well. Maybe you'll be all rested up for some fun in bed at home."

But that was not to be. At home at last and stripped naked of their suits, they tumbled into bed. With his arms around Matt and his hard cock snuggly pressed against him, Bradley slowly fell asleep again.

Matt kissed him on the lips through Bradley's sleepy smile. Then he also drifted off.

Chapter
THREE

MATT sat at the kitchen table the next morning, sipping coffee and playing solitaire on his cell phone. Bradley crept sheepishly into the kitchen and sat down, moving his chair as close to Matt as he could.

"I'm so sorry, honey," Bradley said. He kissed Matt on the cheek and playfully massaged Matt's crotch through his underwear. "Can you ever forgive me for falling asleep at the movies, and just as we were going to make our own love scene? I guess all those late hours at work just finally caught up with me. I'll make it up to you. I promise."

Matt hesitated and looked down at Bradley's hand which had now reached inside Matt's underwear and was massaging Matt's cock which rapidly hardened. "I guess as long as you put it that way," he said with a grin. "A little lower, around my balls, if you don't mind."

Bradley laughed, got down on his knees, took Matt's hardness into his mouth, and swirled the head with his eager tongue.

"There's nothing really to forgive," Matt gasped, "but let's move this back to the bedroom, and I'll let you beg for forgiveness some more anyway."

An eventful and fulfilling hour later, Bradley poured another cup of coffee for Matt and one for himself before joining Matt at the kitchen table once again.

"All better?" Bradley asked.

"You know that it is." Matt beamed. "I've missed that."

"Me too. We're still great together, you know."

"There's no question about that. We just don't have all that much time together very often. And we really can't help that. But we do seem to repeat ourselves all the time."

"Here we go again," Bradley said with a faint smile. "I have this funny feeling I'm going to be sorry I asked, but do you have any suggestions?"

"I was hoping you'd ask," Matt said with a smug grin. "Someone gave me an idea yesterday. I've given some thought to it, and now I'm going to share something with you that sounds pretty crazy."

"Oh yeah? Who's the someone?"

"Clarice." Matt chuckled. Then he added, "Who else?"

Bradley laughed. "Now I understand why you said the idea was pretty crazy. I'm bracing myself so go ahead and tell me what you have in mind."

"Well, here it is..." and Matt proceeded to tell Bradley about the role-play and "cheating" as Clarice had explained it.

Bradley's mouth fell slightly open with surprise, and he stared straight into Matt's eyes. After a few seconds' pause, he said, "Are you serious? Really? You want us to go off to different places and meet but pretend we don't know each other?"

"Think of it as a new game. It might be kind of fun."

"I think you're actually considering doing this."

Matt smiled. "Well, it's really very innocent. We could make up all kinds of fake stories about ourselves and have fun acting out some interesting fantasies. At least we'd be doing different things from just going out to eat and to the movies all the time."

"This is beginning to scare me," Bradley said.

"Scare you? Why?"

"Because it's beginning to sound like something we really might do. That's what scares me."

"Oh, Bradley, you're too serious all the time. It would be sort of like a play, except that we write it ourselves, making it up as we go along. Nobody would get hurt, and we might have an exciting new adventure—whenever we have some time together."

"Let me see if I've got this straight. We meet at a club or a restaurant or someplace, pretend it's by accident, and introduce ourselves as someone else. Like I'm a foreign spy and you're a male prostitute—"

"Wait a minute," Matt protested. "I am *not* going to be some *whore*."

"Why not?" Bradley laughed. "I'd bring cash and pay you really well... *if* you were any good and did the right things to *please me.*"

Matt made a face. "Just for that, I think I might do it. And you better bring a *lot* of money."

"And you'd better be *really good* in bed."

Matt punched Bradley in his left arm. "Bastard."

"Whore."

They both laughed and then hugged.

"We could try it once just to see if we liked the idea," Matt continued. "And if it turned out to be really stupid, at least we would have *tried* something new."

"I guess we could do it once... only to find out if it was fun," Bradley agreed.

"We could start out with something simple. Let me see—I know. What if we went to the public library where Clarice works. Since it was her idea in the first place, I bet she'd like to be on the sidelines to watch. It isn't that far to the Mid-Manhattan Library so we could just zip on over there and try out this idea. We could accidentally meet at one of those big tables in one of the reading rooms and just start up a conversation and see where it goes. If we run into a snag with the librarians, Clarice would be there to help us out."

"What do we do after we introduce ourselves and talk?" Bradley asked with a grin. "Pull out a deck of cards and play Old Maid?" He chuckled at his own idea.

"I don't plan on being an old maid. Anyway, if we decide we like each other... we could go have a drink and maybe get a room in a hotel. It would be like we were really cheating on each other."

Bradley laughed again. "You really would want to go that far with it?"

"It's not like we had anything else planned for tonight. And we don't have to check into the Plaza or some other expensive place."

"I'm *not* a cheap date," Bradley protested.

It was Matt's turn to laugh. "There are lots of moderately priced hotels, you know. Besides, this is just an experiment. If we do it again, we'll get more creative."

"Okay. I guess I'm game for this," Bradley agreed. "You want to do it this afternoon?"

"Sure. I'll call Clarice and see if she wants to meet us there too. It's her day off, but she might be excited to see if this silly idea works. She'd only be a silent observer anyway."

"I guess we're set, then. But we'd better get going since the library closes at six on Saturdays. Call her and let's go. If this charade doesn't work out, you could ask her ahead of time to pretend to be the librarian on duty who throws us out for being naughty. We could signal her or something." Bradley laughed. "She might as well have some fun out of this too. I suppose we'd better go in separate cabs, just to make it more realistic, you know."

"And we'd better wear different clothes from these if we're going to end up on a date."

Bradley smiled wickedly. "That's a very big *if*...."

Matt slugged him in the arm again. "And you'd better stop at an ATM for lots of cash—just in case, of course."

WHEN Matt got to the library reading room, he made a quick tour to see if Bradley had gotten there first. He hadn't. *Maybe he took me seriously and stopped to load up on twenty dollar bills.*

Then he went to the bookshelves and soon found an interesting-looking book on the English Wars of the Roses. "At least I'll have something to read while I wait," he said softly. "And I need a prop anyway to make this look more realistic."

It wasn't long after Matt sat down at one of the tables and began reading his book that he looked up and saw Bradley circling the room looking for him. *Here we go.* Matt resumed perusing his book as though engrossed in the topic.

At last Bradley spotted Matt sitting by himself at a table across the room. He laughed as he walked up to Matt's table and stood directly behind him. "Okay, you little cheat. Let's see how good an actor you are," he said almost inaudibly.

Matt pretended not to hear Bradley and continued reading.

"Hi there," Bradley greeted Matt as he walked around to the other side of the table and stopped. "How's tricks?"

Matt looked up and stared with icy blue-gray eyes into Bradley's twinkling green ones. "I beg your pardon. Were you talking to me?"

"You're the only one here besides me," Bradley said with a smirk.

"Why don't you just move along? I'm busy with my book," Matt said crisply.

"I thought you were supposed to ask me to sit down and then chat with me," Bradley protested.

Matt glared at Bradley. "Play the game, Bradley. Now try again, and do it right."

Visibly taken aback, Bradley cleared his throat and started over. "Uh, excuse me, but is this seat taken?"

"Do you see anyone else around?" Matt asked in a cool low voice.

"You don't have to be so rude about it," Bradley replied. "I just wanted to sit down at a table with a really cute guy."

Matt hid a grin. "Oh. Okay, you can join me, then."

Bradley started to sit across the table from Matt, but then he changed his mind and moved around the table to sit right next to Matt, scooting his chair as close to him as he could.

"Hi," Bradley said, offering his hand. "I'm Charles... uh... Charles Dickens."

Matt rolled his eyes. "Really? How interesting." He shook Bradley's hand. "My name is Bill... Bill Clinton."

Bradley chuckled. "I bet you get kidded a lot about your name."

"No more than you, Chuck. I mean *Charles*. So how are things with David Copperfield and Oliver Twist? Or is that a tale or two that you can't tell?"

"You really are a *smart-ass*, Matt... uh... I mean *Bill*."

"Sorry. I'm new at making small talk with strangers in the library," Matt replied.

"That's okay. Well, uh... do you come here often?" Bradley stammered. "I'm new at this too."

"*No kidding*," Matt replied. "I've only been here a couple of times. How about you?"

"Oh, I've been here lots of times. Actually, I like to come here to look at the cute boys. Maybe you've guessed that I'm gay."

Matt smirked. "I would *never* have guessed. But since you brought it up, I'm gay too."

"Great. Let's go to a hotel together and make *hot love*."

Matt frowned. "I told you, Bradley, *play the game*. You wouldn't really say that to a guy you just met. Work your way up to it."

"Oh, *all right*," Bradley grumbled. "So, Bill, what do you do for a living?"

"That's better," Matt said. "I'm a waiter at one of the Domenico's restaurants. You might have even seen me there. What about you, Charles?"

"I don't really work. I'm independently wealthy. I have some hobbies, but I don't have a real job or anything like that."

Matt's eyes sparkled. "That must be really nice. I have to depend mostly on tips. A waiter's salary isn't very much. I have to hope that rich guys like you... uh... *take care of me*," he said seductively.

At that, Bradley reached into his shirt pocket and pulled out a large wad of twenty-dollar bills and spread them out on the table in front of Matt. "I would just *love* to take care of you, Bill. See anything you like?"

Matt reached out to touch the money, but at that moment a voice behind him said, "Dr. Sharp? Is that you?"

Dumbfounded, Matt jerked his hands back and spun around to see one of his students. His face a bright red, Matt attempted a smile but failed. "Uh... hello, Mr. Andrews. Ah... Derrick, isn't it? What a *surprise* to see you here."

"I live not very far from this library, Dr. Sharp. You know, I really couldn't help overhearing you and this man talking. I didn't know that you worked as a waiter too. And it sounds like this guy is trying to pick you up," Derrick said accusingly as he glared at Bradley.

Matt gulped. "Ah... it's not what you think, Derrick. This is my husband actually, and we're both in a community theater play together. We were just rehearsing."

"Oh," Derrick said, looking greatly relieved. "Wow. You're pretty good. I really believed you were a moonlighting hooker."

"Male escort," Bradley corrected as he gathered up the money and smiled.

"You should let the class know when your play opens so we can all come to see you." chirped Derrick.

"Yeah, Dr. Sharp, you should do that," Bradley said with a sly smile.

"Well, the rehearsals aren't really going that well so it might not get performed after all. I'll let you know if it does," Matt replied.

"Well, I guess I'd better let you two get back to your rehearsal. Keep up the good work. You really had me fooled, Dr. Sharp."

Matt grimaced. "Thanks a lot, Derrick."

"Nice to see you, Dr. Sharp… and I enjoyed meeting you, uh, Bradley was it?"

"That's right," Bradley replied, suppressing a chuckle.

"Good luck with your play. See you in class, Dr. Sharp," Derrick said as he turned and left.

"Quick thinking, Professor," Bradley laughed. "So *now* are you ready to get out of here and head for a hotel, uh… Bill?"

Matt held out a hand. "Give me the money first, Charles, and then we'll go."

Grudgingly, Bradley gave Matt the wad of bills. "I'd better get my money's worth."

"You'll get that and *more than you planned on* if you start griping about the… uh… *escort service* you're about to receive."

Hours later, in a Midtown hotel room bed, Matt cuddled up to Bradley and sighed. Bradley gave Matt a long, lingering kiss.

"So what did you think? Did you enjoy the *cheating*?" Matt asked when their lips finally separated.

Bradley chuckled. "Sure did, Bill. I sure hope my husband, Matt, doesn't find out about this. He'd be jealous that I picked up a good-looking *hunk* like you."

"Did you really enjoy the game? I mean seriously," Matt insisted.

"I have to admit it was a lot more fun than I thought it would be. But my favorite part was the unscripted arrival of your student, Derrick. That made it more than worthwhile."

Matt groaned. "That certainly wasn't fun for *me*. But tell me, do you think you'd want to play another time?"

"Maybe," Bradley said after thinking about it briefly. "Next time we should try someplace a little more exciting than a library."

"Agreed. And the next time we *cheat,* I just hope we don't run into someone we know."

"Come here, Bill. Let's really get our money's worth for this hotel room," Bradley said as he pulled Matt into a naked embrace that brought both their cocks to attention, ready for more. Lips locked, tongues tangled, and limbs entwined, they continued their Saturday night fantasy.

Chapter
FOUR

IT WAS Sunday afternoon, and Bradley sat on the sofa in the apartment. He was reading the national news section of the *New York Times*. Matt was lying on the sofa with his head in Bradley's lap. The magazine section was opened but lying flat on his chest as he soundly slept, not even stirring when Bradley turned pages or switched sections of the paper.

When the knock at the door sounded, Bradley had to carefully move Matt's head onto a throw pillow so he could get up to answer the door. Still Matt did not stir.

Bradley opened the door to find Clarice standing in the hallway.

"Come on in," he whispered and gestured her through the door. "You'll have to keep it down though because Matt's asleep on the couch. Let's go into the kitchen. We can talk there and not wake him up."

She nodded and followed Bradley into the kitchen.

Clarice sat at the table while Bradley poured himself a cup of coffee.

"Want a cup?" he asked.

She shook her head. "Thanks anyway. You go ahead."

Bradley sat down across from Clarice and leaned forward. "Matt's got the right idea. I'm tired too." He yawned, covering his mouth with a hand.

Clarice grinned. "So how come *Bratt* is so tired today? As if I didn't already know the answer to that one."

With tired eyes, Bradley stared at her. "I'm sure you can guess. What happened to you yesterday, anyway? I thought you were going to be at the library when we were there."

"Just as I was about to leave, I got a phone call from my cousin in San Francisco about some family stuff. My mother is a little under the weather. Nothing too serious though. But she kept me on the phone for over an hour. It was nearly six by then so I knew you'd both be gone when I got there. What did I miss? You've just got to tell me all about it."

"Tell you all about what?" Matt asked as he strolled into the kitchen, looking like the cat that ate the canary, or maybe the cat that'd slept all afternoon.

"Oh, don't look so smug, sweetie," Clarice said. "You know exactly what I mean."

"Why don't you ask the *hooker* over there?" Bradley asked as he gestured toward Matt who had joined them at the table. "He's over three hundred dollars richer for the experience."

"What?" Clarice sputtered. She turned to Matt. "Would you please explain that last part to me? I knew about the trip to the library, of course, but I didn't hear anything about money being exchanged."

Matt smiled and paused, milking the moment, and then he told Clarice the story of the male escort "game" she had missed the day before."

"My favorite part was when Matt's student showed up," Bradley said with a chuckle.

"It might not have been so funny if it had been one of your clients from your law firm," Matt retorted with a scowl on his face.

Bradley nodded without comment.

"So that's why you're both so tired today. It all makes perfect sense. Well, did you both enjoy the cheating, so to speak?"

"Yeah," Bradley replied, but then he turned to Matt. "I still don't think you should get to keep all that cash."

"Well, it was your idea that I should play the role of a male escort," Matt retorted.

"I was only joking, and you know it."

"Now, boys," Clarice interrupted. "Let's not fight. It was all for a good cause, after all." She turned to Matt. "But it was just a game, honey. Maybe you should give him the money back."

Matt looked slyly across at Bradley and stared into those green eyes. "I'll think about it."

THE bell rang, and Matt stood up from his desk where he had been sorting some papers from his briefcase. Uncomfortable with restricting himself to the podium at the front of his classroom, he positioned himself to the left of it and prepared to start the day's lecture and discussion. Matt was a roamer. He liked to stroll across the front of the classroom as he talked, and he frequently circled around the entire room, often more than once. His students were careful to stay awake since Dr. Sharp might be close by at any time. Sleepers got asked to leave the class.

"Our topic for today," Matt said as he pointed to the writing on the dry erase board behind him, "is King John of England. You'll notice that he's not King John I, and there's a very good reason for that." Matt paused. "The despicable John Plantagenet was probably the worst king in England's history so in later years no one in the royal family wanted to name a son after him."

Seeing a few eyes already beginning to glaze over, Matt continued. "You probably already know a lot about John. How many of you remember the Robin Hood stories and television shows or movies like *Robin Hood: Prince of Thieves* or even *Robin Hood: Men in Tights*?"

Several hands went up around the room. "Of course, in those stories he was Prince John who ruled in the absence of his older brother King Richard the Lionheart."

Lights began to come on in the eyes of many of the students. "What the Robin Hood stories generally don't tell you is that John did indeed become king upon his brother's death, a few years after Richard returned from the Crusades."

A hand went up from a student near the front of the room.

"Yes, Mr. Connors?"

"Isn't this the same family as in the movie *The Lion in Winter*?"

Matt raised his eyebrows and flashed a warm smile to show his pleasure at the question. "That's really excellent, Mr. Connors. You are indeed right to make that connection. As a matter of fact—"

He was interrupted as the door to the classroom opened, and a student whom Matt did not recognize entered. The student had on a backpack and carried a large card of some sort in his hand. To his surprise, when he finally looked into the student's face as he came nearer, he saw it was Bradley dressed like a college student.

Matt's mouth fell slightly open, and he hesitated a moment, gathering his thoughts. "Can I help you, sir? As you can see, the class has already begun."

Bradley smiled broadly as he walked up to Matt. "Hello, Professor. I'm a new student, but I'm not enrolled for credit. The dean gave me this note," he continued as he handed the card to Matt, "that gives me permission to audit this class."

Matt's eyes narrowed, and he spoke as softly as he could. "What are you up to, Bradley?"

"My name is Percy Plantagenet," Bradley replied cheerfully and loudly enough for the entire class to hear. "And I can't wait to hear your lecture."

"Could I see you in the hall for a moment, Mr. Plantagenet?" Matt said in a deadly calm voice.

"Sure, Professor."

"Class, you may go ahead and visit quietly for a moment until I return. I won't be long."

Bradley followed Matt through the door, and then Matt quietly closed it behind them.

"What do you think you're doing, Bradley?"

"Play the game, Matt. *Play the game*. That's what you told me the first time," Bradley replied, still smiling and winking one of those gorgeous green eyes.

"But we didn't plan this, and besides, *this is my job*," Matt protested.

"Oh, don't take everything so seriously, Matt. I'm not going to embarrass you in front of your kids. In this edition of the game, I'm just a new student who gets a crush on his good-looking professor. Don't you like surprises?"

"I like surprises, but this is a pretty big one."

Bradley leaned over and gave Matt a kiss on the cheek. "Come on. Let's have a little fun, Professor. I won't hurt you."

"And where did you ever come up with a name like *Percy Plantagenet?*" Matt grumbled.

"I saw your notes on the kitchen table last night and got the idea. Did you look at the 'dean's note' I gave you? It's signed by Bugs Bunny."

Matt laughed. "Okay. I give up. But you better be nice in there, and don't interrupt my lesson."

"Can't I even ask any questions if they fit in with the lecture?"

"All right. I guess so, but don't bring too much attention to yourself. It's a good thing Derrick from the library the other day isn't in this class, or he'd probably tell everyone who you really are. By the way, why aren't you at work?"

"Grace gave me a half day off. But I didn't tell her where I was going."

"You better hope I don't pop into your law office with a little role-playing game for *you* one of these days," Matt threatened.

Bradley grinned. "It wouldn't be a surprise now that you've said that. Anyway, we should get back to class, or the students might imagine all sorts of things are going on out here in the hallway," Bradley said before giving Matt another quick kiss on the cheek.

"Behave yourself, Percy, or I'll have to keep you after class and teach you a *private lesson*," Matt said sternly as he reached over and gave Bradley's ass a quick squeeze. Then he winked at him,

"I'm counting on it," Bradley whispered. "*Play the game*, Matt."

Matt nodded and opened the door for them to return to class.

BRADLEY lay in the center of their bed at home, naked. He was partially covered by an equally naked Matt who straddled him at the hips, holding their cocks pressed together. After an hour in bed, however, they had already reached the heights of their pleasure twice so this was now recovery time.

"Did you have a good fantasy, Professor?" Bradley asked with a wide smile.

"I had a great time, Percy, but it wasn't *my* fantasy to seduce a student from one of my classes."

Bradley laughed. "Oh yeah? Then this one would be *mine*. I used to have a crush on my English teacher when I was in high school, and I always wanted to go to bed with him. So I guess this fantasy takes the place of my dream fuck with Mr. Hendrickson. Come to think of it, he was blond and had blue eyes too."

"You're saying that I look like one of your old teachers?" Matt asked. "Is that why you wanted to hook up with me eight years ago?"

Bradley reached up and brought Matt down on top of him so he could kiss him. "No, of course not. That's just a coincidence. I thought you were the cutest guy I'd ever seen when we met. And I still do." He kissed Matt again.

"Well, that's a relief."

"This role-playing stuff is turning out to be really cool. When you first told me the idea, I thought it was kind of dumb, but so far we've had a couple of really interesting adventures."

"We'll have to put our heads together—" Matt began.

"Like we do our dicks?" Bradley interrupted.

It was Matt's turn to laugh. "Sort of, but what I meant to say was that we could figure out some more creative *cheating*, so to speak, if we used our imaginations even more. The library and the classroom were kind of tame."

"I don't think your *classroom* was all that tame. But we had to start somewhere. And with the work schedules we both have, it's not like we can do this every week, you know."

"That's true. But we can toss around some ideas and be ready when we get the chance," Matt suggested. "It does give our lovemaking a fun twist."

"Thanksgiving is coming up before too long, and we'll both have some time off then. Maybe we'll get the chance to continue our role-playing during the holiday."

"Unless Halloween brings something our way first," Matt said with a cheerful grin.

Chapter FIVE

ELLIOT LAWSON was Bradley's straight best friend as well as a fellow junior partner at Grace's law firm, and Bradley loved him almost as much as he loved Matt. They had met as freshmen in college, had shared a dorm room for a year, and had moved into an apartment together their sophomore year. They had even remained in the same shared apartment for the remainder of their undergraduate college days.

When Bradley came out to Elliot that first year, Elliot didn't give it too much thought. But for a day or two, he had made sure he was completely dressed around Bradley because he mistakenly thought that Bradley might be attracted to him. But he had soon realized that that wasn't the case, and he was ashamed of himself for being so silly.

Their mutual respect included their agreement that Bradley stayed away when Elliot was entertaining one of his frequent lady conquests, and Elliot steered clear when Bradley had a guy visiting for the evening. Elliot was sorry to see Bradley go after graduation when he moved in with his then-boyfriend, Matt, but he liked Matt and wished them both well. He'd even flown to California with them for their wedding a few years later, and he had been Bradley's best man.

So it was no surprise when Matt came home one day after classes to find Bradley and Elliot camped out in the living room drinking bottles of beer.

"Doing research for a Budweiser lawsuit?" Matt asked when he saw the collection of bottles on the coffee table.

"No, it's a survey we're filling out that asks how many bottles you can drink before you can't walk anymore," Elliot replied. "But we lost count after six apiece."

"In that case, I'll get you each a large plastic cup to pee in since you probably can't walk to the bathroom," Matt said with a grin. "And don't be embarrassed. I've seen you both naked before."

Elliot looked a little shocked. "And just when did you ever see *me* naked?"

"Remember that time after our wedding in Los Angeles that you had so much to drink you insisted on going swimming in the hotel pool whether or not you had a swimsuit?"

Elliot shook his head sadly and looked away. "Oh yeah. I forgot about that."

"I bet the other guests around the pool will never forget. Bradley, remember that old lady who said she had never seen such a crooked one that hung so far to the side instead of hanging straight down over the balls? She meant your odd-shaped dick, Elliot."

Elliot turned red with embarrassment and involuntarily cupped his crotch.

"Too late, Elliot." Bradley smirked. "We've both already seen it."

"Can we please just change the subject?" Elliot pleaded.

Bradley winked at Matt and said, "Come to think of it, Matt, didn't you have your digital camera that night? And didn't you take a picture of Elliot just before he jumped into the pool?"

"Oh yeah, that's right. I moved it to my old laptop for a screen saver when we got home. Want to see it?"

"What?" Elliot hollered. "You did not. Are you *serious*?"

Matt and Bradley laughed until it hurt.

"We were just kidding," Bradley admitted when he could finally talk again. "But you looked pretty worried there for a minute."

"Wouldn't you? And I repeat, couldn't we please just change the subject?"

Matt headed for the kitchen. "I don't intend to try to catch up with you two, but I *will* join you for a beer. *If* there are any left."

When Matt returned, only Bradley was on the couch. So Matt sat down next to him. "Where's Elliot? Did we scare him off?"

"He's in the bathroom. I guess he really thought you'd hand him a plastic cup to pee in if he didn't go on his own."

Elliot shuffled back to the living room and sprawled onto an easy chair. He turned to Bradley. "Did you tell Matt about my party next week?" he asked.

"I haven't had the chance," Bradley replied. "Why don't you tell him?"

Elliot drained the last of the beer in his bottle, set it on the coffee table, and cleared his throat. "I'm having a Halloween party at my apartment next Saturday night, and this is your official invitation. It's a masquerade party so you can't get in without a costume. Don't forget to wear a mask too."

Matt smiled and clapped his hands. "Oh, good! I just *love* costume parties. And Bradley, didn't I say that maybe something might come up for Halloween?" He winked at Bradley. "You know what I mean," he added in a lowered voice.

Bradley smiled knowingly and nodded. Then he turned to Elliot. "So are you inviting Clarice to the party too?"

"I called her last night. I'm surprised she didn't tell you about the party already."

"Maybe she's just not gotten around to it yet," Matt said. "I know Halloween is her favorite holiday so I bet she's planning a costume already."

"Is there a costume for Ethel Mertz from *I Love Lucy*?" Bradley asked. "That's who she reminds me of when she's buzzing around Matt with some fresh gossip or a new scheme. I even call her that sometimes."

"Hmmm," Matt replied, "I think she's more like Kathy Bates—bold and brassy."

"Oh, I don't know. I see her more as Andy Rooney from *60 Minutes*," Elliot said, laughing. "Before he died, of course. But that's enough of this silly nonsense—let's get back to the point. Are you coming to my party or not?"

"Of course," Matt said, eager to discuss the Halloween party. "What time does it start?"

"Plan to be there after eight thirty or so," Elliot said. "Sometimes there are little kids trick-or-treating in the building, but they're usually finished by that time."

"What's your costume going to be?" Bradley asked. "Or are you keeping it a secret?"

"As a matter of fact, I *am* going to save it as a surprise. That's part of the fun," Elliot replied. Then he looked at his watch. "Wow. It's a lot later than I thought so I need to get going. I'll call a cab and be on my way."

"Don't worry," Bradley said. "Our doorman will get one for you. See you in the office tomorrow."

"I hope I haven't overdone it with the beer. We're not as young as we used to be, Bradley," he muttered as he waved goodbye and closed the apartment door behind him.

Matt turned to Bradley. "So if you think of Clarice as Ethel Mertz, do you see *me* as Lucy Ricardo?"

Bradley laughed. "Not at all. You're my Prince Charming."

"Aw, that's so sweet," Matt replied, and he planted a kiss on Bradley's lips. "But I'm going to feel like Cinderella cleaning house when I have to haul all those beer bottles out of here," he added as he glanced at the mess on the coffee table.

"Don't worry, honey," Bradley said. "It's mostly my mess, and I'll clean it up." He began gathering the bottles.

"I think I'll slip into something more comfortable, like maybe nothing at all, while you're doing that," Matt said. "Meet you in bed as soon as you can get there."

"You bet, sweetie." Bradley picked up the pace and rushed to the kitchen with the bottles.

EARLY Saturday afternoon on the day of Elliot's party, Matt sat on the sofa waiting for Bradley to come out of the bedroom to show off his newly rented costume.

At last Bradley emerged looking like the real Zorro. His black cloth mask tied at the back of his head hid much of his upper face, and the flowing cape looked like something right out of the movies. The black whip even looked rather sinister.

"You look very sexy with all that black. It complements your skin tone and shows that toothpaste-white smile of yours off like you're in a commercial."

"Why, thank you, sir," Bradley replied, trying to snap his whip and make it crack.

"Are you going to wear a little black mustache too?"

"I've got a little pencil-thin one I'll wear at the party. I didn't want to waste the adhesive on a practice run."

"You look shockingly handsome, sweetie."

Bradley blushed a little. "Thanks again. You know, this costume feels so *good*. Maybe I'm the reincarnation of the *real* Zorro."

"Let's not get carried away," Matt said with a grin. "I don't think the original Zorro liked boys, and I doubt he had a husband."

"Now, you don't know that. He might have at least had a boyfriend on the side," Bradley argued.

"Whatever you say. Now it's my turn to dress up. I'll be back in just a few minutes."

While Matt was gone, Bradley took off the hat, mask, and cape, not wanting to wrinkle them or get anything on the costume before the party.

A short time later, Matt returned in his Robin Hood costume. He smiled at the effect it seemed to have on Bradley, whose tongue was hanging out in an exaggerated show of lustful appreciation.

Bradley then gave Matt a spirited wolfish howl and rushed over to hug him. "Wow. You're the best-looking Robin Hood I've ever seen. You're even better than the ones in the movies or on TV. I'm all excited just looking at you. I particularly like how those tights show off your... ah... *figure*."

Matt grinned. "Do you mean my legs or my...?"

"Your face is your best feature," Bradley teased, "but the bulge in your tights is pretty impressive too. It kind of makes me want to reach out and...."

Matt put an arrow into his bow and pretended to aim it at Bradley. "Thanks, but we'll save *some things* for later," he said with a smile. "We aim to please, pun intended."

Bradley laughed. "Come here and give us a kiss."

"Now wait a minute, lover," Matt protested. "Wait until I get out of the costume. I don't want to get it all mussed up before we even *get to the party.*"

"Okay. I guess we ought to hang our costumes back up in the closet until we're ready to go tonight."

When they returned to the living room, they cuddled on the sofa, and Bradley got the kiss he had wanted.

"Now let's plan on how we might play our little game at the party," Matt suggested.

Bradley thought about it for a moment. "I think we should go in the same cab this time, but we could go into the party a few minutes apart. Everybody will be in costume so we'll just pretend we're strangers who've never met before."

"Okay," Matt agreed, "and since we already know what each other's costume looks like, we can just casually approach each other and take it from there."

"Sounds like a good plan. Anything else we can just make up as we go along, and nobody will notice or even care because they'll all be busy partying anyway."

"Are you going to make up a fake name again?"

"Of course," Bradley replied. "We're supposed to be strangers, you know."

"Okay. I'll think about one too," Matt said.

Bradley gave him another kiss. "Don't think *too* hard. I don't want Robin Hood to be too tired to party. Especially later after the *official* party."

THAT night when Bradley and Matt got off the elevator in Elliot's apartment building, they stopped before going down the hallway to the party.

Bradley adjusted his Zorro mask and pressed firmly on his newly applied thin mustache. Then he turned to Robin and said, "You go ahead first while I put on my cape. I didn't want to wear it in the cab and get it wrinkled."

"You're lucky the cab driver let you into the cab at all with that big black whip," Robin replied.

"Me? You're the one who was lucky to get into the cab since you were carrying that bow with all those arrows. It looks like the real thing and not a toy at all."

"Well, it doesn't matter since he made us put it all in the trunk anyway."

"Get going," Zorro insisted. "I'll finish with this cape, wait a few minutes, and then I'll come inside and look for you."

"At least give me a chance to get a drink before you get there," Robin said. "I'm kind of thirsty."

Zorro gave Robin a little shove and sent him on his way to the party. After he put on his cape, he practiced cracking his whip and nearly smacked Little Bo Peep and the Easter Bunny who were getting off the elevator and heading for Elliot's place.

"Oops! Sorry!" Zorro said. "I didn't see you coming."

"It's okay," the Easter Bunny replied. "No harm done. I'm rather into S and M—myself."

Zorro waited for about five more minutes, during which time Darth Vader and the Queen of Hearts got off the elevator holding hands. Then he headed off down the hall and knocked on Elliot's door. He could hear the party music very clearly from within.

Alice in Wonderland opened the door. "Come on in, Zorro." She eyed the whip and said, "I don't know about *horses* to use that thing on, but there are a few *asses* here at this party."

Zorro laughed. "I'll look them up." He cracked the whip, causing a few people to jump and then look at him worriedly.

Once inside, Zorro was a little shocked at how many people were there. It was a lot more crowded than he had expected, and he didn't see Robin Hood yet. It was also a lot darker than he thought it would be, and he found himself bumping into characters of all kinds. The devil gave him an ugly stare when Zorro accidentally tromped on his tail, but Zorro hurriedly moved on.

Zorro found the bar and poured himself a cup of punch. He took a sip and choked, making an ugly face. "Ugh! This is terrible stuff! It's got gin in it. I hate gin. Somebody must have poured this into the fruit punch thinking it was rum or vodka," he groaned, examining the two unmarked decanters on the bar. He sniffed each one.

Sure enough, the empty one smelled like gin, and the half-full one next to it obviously smelled of rum. "I bet Elliot doesn't even know what happened." He set the cup back on the counter and moved in a circle around the packed living room. He still didn't find Robin Hood.

Following a fat Humpty Dumpty who cleared the way for him, Zorro headed to the hall near the bedroom. Partygoers had spilled into the open bedroom, and Zorro wasn't really surprised to see some couples coming close to turning the room into an orgy. But their costumes kept them from going too far since many of them were too awkward to permit sprawling on the bed.

Back in the hallway again, Zorro finally found Robin.

"There you are," Zorro said. "I've been looking everywhere for you."

"Really?" Robin replied. "Well, I've been looking for such a handsome Zorro all my life."

Zorro grinned. "You found me." He leaned over and kissed Robin.

Robin grinned wickedly and threw his arms around Zorro, up under the cape. Then he gave Zorro a deep, soulful kiss that caused a stirring in Zorro's crotch.

"Wow. You sure know how to kiss all right."

Since it was fairly dark in the hallway, Zorro figured no one else would notice what he was doing. He reached down to the crotch of Robin's tights and began to massage it. He wasn't surprised that Robin's cock rapidly increased in size. Actually, Zorro was amused at how big it got. But he enjoyed the sensation since Robin was returning the favor and rubbing him back through his tight pants.

Catching his breath, Zorro said, "I forgot to introduce myself. My name is Dick Placid."

"It doesn't feel very *placid* to me."

"Ha ha," Zorro said. "Very funny. You know very well I meant that was my *name*."

Robin snickered. "I was making an editorial comment. Okay, Dick. It's nice to meet you. My name is Guy Pearce, like the movie star."

"Oh really? Does that mean you have piercings? Like your tongue, or your navel, or maybe even your dick?" Zorro teased.

Robin smiled wickedly again. "That's up to you to find out, Dick." With that remark, Guy pulled Dick's hand up under his green tunic and down inside his tights where Dick felt a throbbing hot cock. Oddly, it felt somehow unfamiliar in his fingers.

"There you are," a familiar voice called. "I've been around this apartment three or four times looking for you."

Zorro turned around and was stunned to see another Robin Hood. He quickly pulled his hand out of the first Robin's tights and felt a thudding in his chest. His blood felt like ice in his veins. *Uh-oh! This can't be good.*

As Matt moved nearer to him, Bradley examined the other Robin more carefully, and he was amazed at the almost-identical blond hair and similar body build. He could be looking at Matt's brother, if he had one.

Matt also had seen the quick movement of Zorro's hand away from the other Robin's costume. "What exactly are you doing, Bradley? Why was your hand inside this guy's pants?"

"His name isn't Bradley. You've made a mistake. He *says* his name is Dick Placid," the other Robin said.

"Oh, I just bet his dick *isn't* placid either," Matt retorted.

Bradley looked from one Robin to the other and then back at his own Robin. "Look, sweetheart, it was all a simple mistake. It's dark back here in the hall, and I just assumed this was you."

Matt looked very carefully at the other Robin again, and then he smiled at Bradley. "Well, I admit that in that costume he does look a lot like me. And I know it's kind of dark. But wasn't there *something* you found a little different? And you *know* what I mean."

"Uh... his *nose* wasn't shaped exactly like yours?" Bradley stammered.

"Give me a break."

The first Robin interrupted. "Look, if you two are a couple or something, I'll take off. But I thought you were beginning to like me," he said to Bradley.

"I thought you were him." He pointed to Matt. "I'm really sorry about this mix-up."

"Oh, that's okay, I guess." The other Robin turned to Matt. "You're lucky to have a hunk like him. If you decide you don't want him after all...."

"Never mind," Matt replied. "He messed up, but he's still mine, and I'll keep him."

"Well, happy Halloween," the stranger Robin said softly as he went back to the party.

"I'm really, really sorry, Matt," Bradley said. "Please don't be mad."

Matt laughed. "I'm not mad. Now that I think about it, it's pretty funny."

Bradley breathed a sigh of relief. "Really? You're okay with all this?"

"I'm not happy you had your hand in his pants playing with his dick, but I understand the mistake. But seriously, you couldn't tell he wasn't me?"

Bradley thought about telling Matt that the other guy's dick was indeed bigger, but he decided not to press his luck. "Honestly, Matt, I couldn't tell the difference."

"Ahem. Dark as it is in here, I could still see his crotch. You're lying, but I love you for it."

Bradley just smiled innocently.

"This could only happen to us," Matt added. "I guess we had it coming for playing our little *cheating* game at a party. We'll have to be more careful in the future."

"You're absolutely right, sweetheart," Bradley agreed. Then he looked around the large living room. "I wonder what happened to Clarice."

"I'm right here," Alice in Wonderland said. "You didn't recognize me, did you? Neither one of you did."

"You're right," Matt agreed. "Not with that clunky mask you're wearing. Where have you been all this time?"

"Well, for the last ten or fifteen minutes, I've been watching a real soap opera. It was the story of two Robins, a Zorro, and a hand in the wrong place."

Bradley turned red, Matt giggled, and the Burger King laughed.

"Elliot!" Bradley, Matt, and Clarice shouted at the same time.

"It's *you*," Bradley said.

Standing next to them, previously unnoticed, was a plastic face familiar from old TV commercials. He removed his plastic head and said, "Thanks for coming to my party. I loved your side show best of all."

"I didn't even see you at all this entire evening. Where have you been?" Bradley asked.

"I was just wandering around watching my guests when I saw Zorro here getting chummy with Robin Hood. So I watched until the other Robin arrived on the scene. It just got better from there."

"I'm glad everyone had such a good time at my expense," muttered Bradley.

Elliot smiled. "It probably wouldn't have happened if you two hadn't been in the middle of that role-playing game Clarice suggested."

"You knew about that?" Bradley asked. "That's a surprise. I didn't think anyone else knew—"

"Clarice told me about it. Now let's all go get a drink and dance a little," Elliot suggested.

"Do you have anything besides that awful punch?" Clarice asked.

"There's beer in the kitchen. Come on. Let's party."

Chapter
SIX

McKENNA AND ASSOCIATES occupied two floors of a large office building in Manhattan. In addition to some conference rooms for the use of its clients and associates, there were several senior associates' offices and cubicles for junior partners. There was also one large meeting room on the upper floor near Grace McKenna's office.

The senior partners were concluding a meeting there, but Grace was on her way out since she had completed her part of the discussion. She closed the door firmly behind her, thus muting the buzz of conversation still going on. She carried three fairly thick file folders and she wore a look of concern.

Grace was proceeding to her office for a private meeting with one of the partners. First, however, she wanted to review some of the vital information in those folders.

On the way to her office, she passed the smaller spaces where the firm's junior partners labored each day. She glanced at her employees until she spotted Bradley going into his office. He looked around in time to see her smile at him and wave a greeting. He waved back.

When she got to her office, she stopped at her secretary's desk. "Marge, in about fifteen minutes I'd like for you to call Winston Kirby to my office. He knows what it's about. Just buzz me when he arrives. And don't put through any calls either before or during my meeting with Winston."

"Of course, Ms. McKenna," Marge replied. "Can I get you anything first?"

Grace smiled. "You're so good to me, Marge, and I sincerely appreciate all that you do. But I don't need anything just now. Thanks just the same." Grace strolled into her office and quietly closed the door.

Grace laid the folders on her desk, located the pages with the figures that she wanted to study, and hardly looked up until several minutes later when Marge called her on the desk phone.

"Mr. Kirby is here."

"Send him right in, please."

Winston Kirby entered the office and stood inside the door for a moment. She looked up and signaled him to sit in the chair facing her desk.

"Good morning again, Winston," Grace began. "Did the meeting conclude in good order?"

"Yes, it did," he replied. "And before you even ask, I'll tell you that no one has a hint of what's about to happen. At least there's been no obvious sign that anyone suspects anything at this point. I can usually tell if there have been some rumors floating around. Concerning anything important, that is. There's always a little gossip of some sort going on between the junior and senior partners. That's pretty common."

"Good," Grace remarked. "Soon enough we're going to have to tell everyone our big news, but I'd rather save it for an official announcement when everyone will have to make some major decisions."

Winston nodded. "I agree. There's no point in stirring them all up too soon."

Grace pointed to the papers on her desk. "I've been studying these projections, and I think you and I should make some preliminary decisions of our own. Since we're going to expand the firm and establish a second office in Los Angeles, I think it's pretty obvious that we're going to have to cut our staff in half here in New York and send the others, those who would agree to make the move, to the new office out West. You, of course, will head the New York office when I've moved to the new one. I'm going to give you the opportunity to decide if there are some partners and associates that you'd particularly like to keep here with you. That assumes both their approval and mine, of course."

"Naturally," Winston concurred. "I won't ask to keep anyone you consider vital to the new branch office. I guess it's a matter of looking at the list of our personnel and making some preliminary selections."

Grace chuckled. "You mean like choosing sides to play a baseball game?"

"In a very specialized way, I guess, but as we've discussed, this is actually going to be rather premature because ultimately it will be up to the individuals whether they want to stay or move out West."

"That's true," Grace agreed.

"But I think that each of us might have a preference for which partners we would like to have stay with us. Let's just look at it that way, if that's all right with you."

"You're such a diplomat, Winston. I believe that you're trying to tell me you have a favorite or two." She smiled.

"One or two," Winston admitted.

Grace continued, "However, when we ask for preferences, the division between the two branches may not turn out to be even. If more than half want to stay rather than go, we're going to have to revisit the list to see which ones must be let go. We simply can't afford to keep more than half of our employees in either branch."

"I hope that doesn't happen. We'd be writing some letters of reference in that case. Not to mention that we'd have to scramble out in LA to hire some new employees."

"And we can't send more than half to California. Some are going to have to stay here, like it or not. At least for the time being." Grace frowned slightly.

"There's another thing," Winston injected. "Do we really have the resources to pay the moving expenses for this many people? It's going to cost a fortune."

Grace gulped. "We can cover it, but it's the least incentive that we can offer, considering the higher cost of living in California for our employees. We had *better* make this work, Winston. A lot of our reserves are on the line here. But I've always believed that you have to spend money to make money."

"Well, we're certainly going to *spend* money."

"And let's not forget a major consideration. Anyone on the advance team had better get busy studying to pass the bar in

California," she added. "And *fast* if we're going to start up next year. Maybe we can start some study sessions and form some groups to help prepare for the bar out there. We'll be able to plan better when we know who's going."

"That's true, but the first ones out there will merely be doing things like finding office space and setting up the details. There will be a longer time for the rest to take care of it later."

MATT opened his apartment door to let Clarice inside. "Can I get you a beer or something?" he asked. "I was just about to get myself a drink."

"How about just a soft drink over ice? Anything diet will do."

"Fine. I'll be right back."

Clarice waited for Matt to return with the two drinks. Then she began deliberately walking around the living room as though examining the walls.

"What on earth are you doing, Clarice?" Matt asked. "Looking for blood on the walls?"

"Funny you should say that," she replied with a grin. "I was looking for any holes or punctures."

"Huh?"

"More specifically—arrow holes in the wall. I thought perhaps that after you two got home from Elliot's party you might have started shooting arrows at Bradley after that really funny Robin Hood mix-up."

"Very funny, Clarice. I wasn't mad at Bradley. It was just an honest case of mistaken identity. It could have happened to anybody."

"Particularly to anybody who was playing a little game of *cheat on your husband* at a Halloween party."

Matt smiled ruefully. "I think we've about exhausted this topic of conversation."

"Okay. Then how is *Bratt* doing this week?"

"*Bratt* is just fine," Matt assured her. "If you hang around a little longer, you'll see that for yourself. Bradley isn't going to be late today. He called earlier to let me know."

"Good. I really haven't seen that much of him lately, except in a black mask with a black hat and carrying a big black whip." Clarice took a sip of her drink, but she looked troubled.

"So what's up? To what do I owe the honor of this afternoon's visit? You don't look very cheerful today."

"Can you really tell?" she asked.

"You just don't look very happy. Is something wrong?"

"Well, yes. Remember that time I got a call from a cousin about my mother in San Francisco?"

Matt nodded. "Did something else happen to your mother?"

"She had a little stroke yesterday. She's responding pretty well, and it doesn't look like there is any permanent damage, but it *was* a stroke after all."

Matt jumped up and rushed to hug Clarice. "I'm so sorry, Clarice. You must be terribly worried."

"Well, it could have been a lot worse. But it scared me a little so I'm going to fly out to California to spend some time with her and my cousin. It's been several months since I was there. Anyway, I just wanted to let you know where I'll be for a week or so."

Matt kissed her on the cheek. "I'll miss you, but your mother will be so glad to have you there. I hope you'll call every day or two and let us know how it's going."

"Oh, I will. And please tell Bradley for me, won't you?"

"You know that I will."

Clarice set her glass on the coffee table and rose to leave. "I need to get packed because I'm on a flight in the morning. See you later, Matt."

Matt hugged her again and gave her another kiss on the cheek. "You take care, and we'll talk soon."

Matt sat back down on the sofa after she had left. *I'm really going to miss her....*

His thoughts were interrupted by a knock at the door.

"I wonder what she forgot," Matt murmured as he headed for the door.

Matt was shocked when he opened the door. It was an AmeriPost delivery man with a large shipping box. The man wore the standard white shirt with a red tie and blue short pants. A little red-and-white AmeriPost oval patch was sewn neatly on his shirt with his name in small letters at the bottom of the oval—Tom Cruise. But the delivery man was Bradley.

"Package delivery," Bradley sang out cheerfully. "Dr. Matthew Sharp? Is that you, sir?"

Matt was so surprised it took him a moment to gather his wits. "Uh… yes, that's me. Where did you get that uniform?"

"Play the game, Matt. Play the game."

"Uh… okay. Your name is Tom Cruise? How come you don't look like you do in the movies?"

Bradley beamed. "Oh, the name's just a coincidence. But before they changed his hair and put in colored contact lenses, the actor looked just like me. I'm better looking, of course."

Matt laughed this time. "Yes, I'm *sure* that I see what you mean. And you're so *modest* too." Matt grinned at 'Tom'. "Won't you come in? That package looks very heavy."

"Thank you, I will," Tom replied as Matt closed the door. "But this isn't really heavy at all. See?" He handed it to Matt.

"You're right," Matt agreed. "It's a lot lighter than it looks."

"Who sent it?" Tom asked. "Is the name on the return address?"

Matt looked more carefully at the handwritten label. "Hmmm. It says it's from someone named Percy Plantagenet. I believe I vaguely remember that name." He gave Tom an amused stare. "He's one of my former students. I think he was a slower student who *failed* my class."

Tom smirked. "Why don't you open it up, sir? Aren't you curious about the contents?"

Now it was Matt's turn to smile broadly at the delivery man. "Why, Tom. I'm surprised a delivery man like you would stay long enough to see what was in someone's package."

"It's my last delivery of the day, sir, and my curiosity has just gotten the best of me. I wonder what's so light that takes such a big box."

"I just love *big packages*. Don't you, Tom?" Matt stared directly as Bradley's crotch which the tight little blue shorts outlined perfectly. "Do you have a big package, Tom?"

Tom beamed again. "I don't like to brag, sir, but I'm told that it's impressive."

"Really?" Matt asked. "Do you suppose that you would mind showing me?"

Tom grinned. "Sure. Just as soon as you've opened that up. Then I want to see *your* package too. Uh… I meant to say that I wanted to see what's *inside* your package." He was almost laughing.

Matt took the box into the living room and opened it on the floor by the sofa. Tom watched very intently. Inside was something rather bulky wrapped with layers and layers of white tissue paper. Matt unwound and unwound sheet after sheet. Finally he was left with a much smaller box.

Tom merely smiled and waited.

Matt opened the box to find the largest sex toy he had ever seen. Tom burst out laughing.

"If you think for one minute that I'm going to—" Matt began.

"I thought you wanted to see my package," Tom interrupted, quickly slipping off his blue shorts and underwear as Matt stared and grinned. "Like what you see?"

Matt felt his cock enlarge rapidly. "You bet, Tom. Come on into the bedroom and I'll show you mine. But we're leaving *that thing* out here."

Brad smiled wickedly. "Whatever you say."

LATER as they lay cuddled in bed, Matt remarked, "For someone who was reluctant to play the game at first, you've certainly jumped right in."

"It turns me on, just like *you* turn me on, sweetie," Bradley replied. "I had no idea this was going to be so much fun."

"Where did you get that AmeriPost uniform? It looks like the real thing."

"Most of it I just made up with stuff I found at a store—the shirt, shorts, and tie were easy. But I had to have the name patch custom-made at a novelty shop. The guy was reluctant to sew the name of a real business on it, but I talked him into it."

"*And just how* did you do that?" Matt asked, already knowing the answer.

Bradley laughed. "I just smiled a lot, winked a few times, and assured him it was just for a little joke. I also mentioned that no one would know where the patch came from anyway."

"Since Thanksgiving is coming up pretty soon, have you thought up any new ideas for when we're on vacation from work for a few days?"

"Now that you mention it, there is one idea I've been mulling over," Bradley said. "It's a lot more elaborate than anything we've done yet, but it might be kind of thrilling."

"Tell me about it. It sounds exciting already."

"Well, I have to tell you right from the beginning. My idea could be a little dangerous. But I don't think we would really get into trouble."

"Uh oh. You're making me a little nervous," Matt said. "You'd better explain your idea."

"I thought we might pretend to conduct a drug deal... at a gay biker bar... and then decide we turned each other on and take off together."

"*What*?" Matt exploded. "Are you *crazy*? A drug deal? We could get arrested."

"Now hear me out, sweetheart. It's not as bad as it sounds. The cocaine would really be plastic bags of powdered sugar in a backpack, and the money would just be play money in a briefcase. I'd go in first as the buyer and wait for you, the seller, to come in. We'd make a deal in the back and go off together. No one would get hurt."

"Wait a minute. I thought I heard you say something about a gay biker bar. That sounds pretty extreme. And you know where to find one?"

"It's rare, but trust me. I googled it under *gay biker bars* and found one here in New York."

Matt tilted his head. "If you say so—"

Bradley laughed. "It would make the whole thing feel more realistic. Besides, if we went to a straight bar, we might draw too much attention."

Matt was incredulous. "You think trading a backpack for a briefcase in the back of *any* bar would be inconspicuous?"

"Well, it's unlikely that the cops or the Feds would be in a gay biker bar, and the customers would probably ignore us."

"Oh sure. We go in there without leather and chains... or whatever else they wear in a place with bikers... and no one will notice."

Bradley was undaunted. "I guess they *might* notice us, but we'd certainly look harmless, and nobody would look at us after the first few minutes."

"I don't know about this, Bradley," Matt replied. "It sounds awfully risky. Pretending to sell cocaine in a bar like that... it might be just a little too over-the-top."

"Where's your sense of *adventure*, Matthew? Don't you want to do something *daring*?"

"I keep picturing things like getting *arrested*, getting *fired*, getting *killed*...."

Bradley laughed again. "Sweetheart, you're just being too melodramatic. Nothing's going to happen to us."

"It sounds like you've got this planned out to the last detail."

"Yeah. I gave it a lot of thought. The one I found is in a neighborhood that's kind of bad, but we'll be careful. And we won't be there but for a few minutes anyway."

"What's the name of the place?" Matt asked.

Bradley looked a little sheepish. "Uh... well, it's called Killer Joe's."

"Oh, that's just fine. It'll look colorful in our obituaries in the *Times*."

MATT turned to Bradley and squealed, "This is all *your* fault."

"How did I know anyone would watch us?" Bradley protested. "It seemed like a good idea—"

"Enough pulling each other's hair, girls," the leader interrupted. "We're going to take a little trip together. But don't you worry your pretty little heads. It won't be a long one. Now get up and walk slowly and carefully with us to the back exit by the restrooms. We'll go to the alley that way." He waved his knife at them menacingly as they shakily got out of their chairs.

As they reached the restrooms, one of the men said, "Spike, maybe we should let the girls go to the ladies' room before we leave. You know," he said as he winked at the leader, "for the *last time*."

The leader winked back. "You're right, Crusher. It wouldn't be decent of us to let them piss all over themselves and their clothes as they're dying in the alley. We're better than that. Okay, girls. Step right into the ladies' room over there and let it go for the last time. No funny business now. We'll be here watching the door." He struggled to keep from laughing.

Bradley and Matt looked at each other and nodded.

"We promise," Matt squeaked.

"And don't take too long. Otherwise, we'll think you're doing each other one last time."

One of the men in back snickered softly.

As quickly as they could, Matt and Bradley rushed into the ladies' room and locked the door behind them, not hearing the chuckles outside the door.

"What a stroke of luck," Matt exclaimed. "We've got a chance to get out of here."

Bradley looked around and saw the window. "If we're quick, maybe we can get out through that window and down the alley. Surely we can escape before they realize we're gone."

Matt tried the window. "It's going to take both of us to get it open."

With four hands pushing, they finally got the window open as wide as it would go.

"You go first, Matt, and then I'll be right behind you."

"Okay. Here I go," Matt whispered as he climbed through the window and dropped the short distance to the alley. "Come on, Bradley."

Bradley hoisted himself up and scrambled through the window. "Let's get out of here *right now*."

In the shadows of the alley outside the back door of the bar, the four bikers watched in delight as the two escapees ran down the alley like third-grade girls running home from school. When Bradley and Matt reached the end of the alley and turned the corner, they burst into loud laughter.

ONCE back inside the bar, the men sat down at the table where Bradley and Matt had sat a few minutes earlier.

"Crusher, you count the money, and I'll test the quality of this cocaine," Spike said.

Crusher opened the briefcase, but as he started to take out the money he exclaimed, "Spike! This is nothing but *play money*. We've been *robbed*."

"I've got more bad news, boys," Spike replied as he put his finger into one of the bags and put it to his tongue. "This stuff is just powdered sugar. It's not coke at all. Those guys pulled a fast one on *us*. And we thought we were the ones who were playing games with *them*. Son of a bitch. What's going on here? Who are these guys that set us up like that?"

MATT and Bradley were nearly out of breath having run three blocks from the bar. They stopped to rest in a side street, anxiously looking over their shoulders to see if they were being followed.

"Bradley, you better call Elliot or somebody to come in a cab to get us. We'll *never* find a cab at night in this part of town."

"I'm on it already," Bradley replied as he punched a number into his cell phone. "It's ringing. Elliot? It's me, Bradley. I need you to get a cab and come get Matt and me. And I mean *right now*. We're in some trouble. Can you help us? Okay, here's where we are." He looked up at a street sign so he could tell Elliot their exact location.

"MATT, sweetheart, come on. Don't be *mad*," Bradley begged as the cab sped away.

Matt sat by the window and simply glared at Bradley.

"You have to speak to me sometime, you know."

"No, I don't," Matt snapped and continued glaring.

"See? You did say something to me. That wasn't so hard, was it?"

The silence was so great you could hear the faint ticking of the meter in the front seat of the cab.

"Can I ask a question?" Elliot said, breaking the silence.

"No," Matt and Bradley said at the same time.

"Do you smell something kind of funny back here?" Elliot asked from his side of the cab. "It kind of smells like piss."

"Shut up, Elliot!" Bradley barked. "Nobody asked you."

"Now that you mention it," Matt replied. "I think I do smell—"

"We'll talk about it when we get home, Matt. Now I don't see why you're all that mad anyway. We got out *alive*. We didn't even get hurt. We lost some powdered sugar and play money, but that's certainly no big deal," Bradley tried again.

Matt stared stonily ahead. Then without warning he muttered, "We lost my backpack and my briefcase."

Bradley couldn't help it. He laughed. Then he saw the look in Matt's eyes and said, "Sweetie, those things don't really matter, and you know it. The important thing is that we got out of there in one piece."

Matt looked across at Elliot who sat silently. Then he drew a deep breath. "I told you from the very beginning that this idea was too dangerous. It was too *over-the-top*, and I told you that too. But you didn't listen. You had to do something *thrilling* and *exciting*, even though it could have gotten us both killed."

"Now be fair, Matt. You know you liked the idea when we discussed it. And we did kind of have fun this evening."

"Oh yeah. It's a lot of fun to have somebody pull a knife on you and threaten to kill you with it. And I had a lot of laughs climbing out of that ladies' room window and running down the alley for my life. You're right. I couldn't have asked for a *better time* for Thanksgiving."

"Did anyone ever tell you how pretty your blue eyes get when you're sarcastic like that?" Bradley smiled.

Once again Matt glared at him.

Bradley reached over and took Matt's hands into his. "Matt, honey, I really *am* sorry. I didn't have any idea that those goons would be there and give us such a hard time. Could I point out something to you? They must have known we'd climb out that window when they let us go in there. Hell, they're the ones who insisted that we go into the restroom in the first place. I bet they just wanted to scare us so we wouldn't come back to that bar."

"Like we would," Matt snapped.

"But you see what I mean, don't you, sweetie? They weren't going to hurt us. They were just having some fun at our expense."

Matt thought about it for a few minutes and stared at Bradley. "You really think that?"

"Sure I do. If they were going to kill us, they'd have marched us outside to the alley and they would have just done it. You noticed that no one came running after us."

"That's true," Matt admitted. "I guess you're right when you put it that way. Still, it was scary and I almost wet my pants when that guy started waving that knife around."

"I can beat that, honey. I *did* wet my pants," Bradley admitted. "Want to feel my crotch to see where I'm still damp?"

"I knew I was right about that!" Elliot interjected.

It was Matt who laughed, though. "Really? You *did*? Oh, Bradley, I'm sorry I laughed. I didn't mean to hurt your feelings."

Bradley smiled. "That's okay. I'm just glad you're feeling better. I can tell I've got my Matt back when you laugh like that. I love you, sweetie."

"I love you too."

"I wish I could have seen their faces when they tried the cocaine and saw the money."

"Me too." Then Matt leaned over and kissed Bradley before timidly reaching down to feel Bradley's crotch.

"Oh Bradley. It really *is* still wet."

"I told you so," Bradley laughed again. "Let's take off our clothes when we get home, take a quick shower, and go to bed. Then let's just forget about the whole thing."

"Okay," Matt agreed, "but I *would* like to tell Clarice about it when she gets back from San Francisco. Especially the part about you wetting your pants."

"Please, Matt," Bradley begged. "Leave that part out."

Matt was silent for a moment. At last he said, "Okay, Bradley. I'll think it over."

"Hey, you two. We're at your apartment building," Elliot announced as the taxi came to a halt. "I'll pay the cabbie when I get home, and you can settle up with me later...."

Chapter SEVEN

GRACE stood at the imposing podium in the large meeting room and looked over the associates and various partners who had gathered for the morning's all-staff meeting. Some sat whispering quietly with others while quite a few sat and stared back at her in silence. Most of them appeared to be in shock at the news she had just delivered about the new branch in Los Angeles.

To break the silence, Grace said, "Are there any questions? Though I realize asking that is ridiculous because you *all* must have many, many questions. I suggest that you let it all sink in before you panic or cheer or scream." She smiled in what she hoped was a reassuring way.

"I know my announcement is a complete surprise, but look at it this way. Here is an opportunity for some of you to move to the West Coast, if that's something that you would like to consider. It's Hollywood, movie and television studios, celebrities everywhere, the entertainment capital of America, Disneyland, and a totally different landscape and lifestyle from what you know here."

She looked around the room at some skeptical faces and laughed. "And yes, I know that it's also smog, crowded freeways, and a higher cost of living too. But it's also a chance for the excitement and challenge of creating a new firm as well as advancing in your careers because of the seniority you already have.

"Or it's a chance to stay here in New York and help build the firm back up to our current size, but you would also have that same seniority in your quest for advancement. It's really something exciting and rewarding, whichever way you choose to look at it."

A hand went up in the back of the room. "What if not enough of us want to move? Would you elaborate on that a little? You've said that the firm will only be half the current size in either branch until it builds back up again, which will take a few years. And yet you also said we didn't have to go to LA if we didn't want to."

Grace hesitated. "You've seized upon the only downside to this expansion to the West Coast. If too many of you want to stay here, we can't afford to keep the same size staff in New York. In that case, we'll have to let some of you go.

"I regret that deeply, but we will give you the best possible references to help you find a position with a different firm. Perhaps this knowledge might help some of you decide to go ahead and move, but I'm certainly not suggesting that we'll be trying to force you into something you absolutely do not want to do." Grace could see the confusion, and in some cases bewilderment, on the faces of her staff.

"Think it over, discuss it with your families, and then we'll see where we stand with the numbers. However, I *do* need your decision in about two weeks at the latest. We must begin our planning so we can open the new firm in the early spring of next year."

At last there was a noticeable undercurrent of whispering among the staff. Another hand went up. "Is there a limit for the moving expenses for those who choose to go?"

"That's an excellent question, but the figure allotted will depend on a number of factors, including how many are in a staff member's family. It's not an exact number, and we'll work with you individually on that. We'll also try to help find affordable housing. Anything else?"

No more hands went up so Grace concluded the meeting, and employees slowly got up to go back to work. Finally, she could tell that there was at least *some* excitement in various voices as conversations began about her stunning announcement.

BRADLEY had been sitting next to Elliot during the meeting so the two of them headed back to their cubicles.

"Wow. Wasn't that a surprise?" Elliot asked. "Did you see this coming?"

"Totally unexpected," Bradley replied. "*Los Angeles*. Who would have thought Grace had an idea like that in her head?"

"I know. So what do you think? Are you interested in moving to California?"

"I don't know what to say. I'm a New Yorker, and I thought I always would be. It never entered my mind to live in California. Besides, there's Matt to consider. I need to take into account what he thinks about this. It isn't just my decision, you know."

Elliot nodded. "I'm sure Matt will have a lot to say about this."

Bradley laughed. "Oh, he *will*. He's never shy about his opinions. You can count on that. What about you?"

Elliot frowned. "I'm not sure. I always thought I would stay in New York. But in a way, the idea sort of appeals to me. I don't know. I'll have to think about it. On the other hand, I couldn't leave you and Matt. You two *depend* on me so much." He laughed, and so did Bradley.

WINSTON approached Grace as she made her way out of the conference room and headed toward her office. "I think that it went fairly well, all things considered."

"At least no one stood up and started *yelling*...."

"Or *cheering* either," Grace finished for him. "It's too soon to tell what they really think or how they will respond."

"Yes, of course. But at least it's a start. I'll visit with you later, Grace," Winston said. "Elliot Lawson is just over there in his cubicle with Bradley Moore, and I want to speak to Elliot about something."

Grace smiled. "I think I can guess why. I bet you want to keep him, if you can. See you later."

Winston strode quickly toward Bradley and Elliot. "Good morning, gentlemen," he greeted them with a smile. "Mr. Lawson, could I please have a word with you in my office?"

"Of course, Mr. Kirby," Elliot replied. "See you later, Bradley," he said as he followed Winston.

"Have a seat, Elliot." Winston ushered him toward a chair as he closed the door. He sat at his desk and looked directly into Elliot's eyes. "Well, what do you think about our grand announcement this morning?"

"It's a shock, Mr. Kirby. I don't know how else to put it."

"Let's drop the formalities, Elliot. You can call me Winston."

Elliot looked a little bewildered, but he nodded.

"I think I'll get straight to the point. Where do you think you'd prefer to be—here or in Los Angeles?"

"I really don't know, sir. I mean, *Winston*. I was just talking to Bradley about that very thing. I've visited California, but I always assumed I'd stay in New York."

Winston smiled. "You're not itching to go out and mingle with the stars in Hollywood?"

Elliot laughed. "There are lots of stars in New York, so I don't guess so."

"I'm very glad to hear you say that, Elliot. I want to discuss a little proposition with you. As you know, I'll be taking Grace's place when she leaves next spring, and I'd like to offer the opportunity to put you on the fast track to become a senior partner, here in New York."

Elliot's eyes grew wide, and he smiled. "Really, Winston? That would be terrific."

"And a clear path to sharing some real responsibilities around here. I'm sure you realize the implications of that. It's not an inconsiderable offer."

"Wow. I was already shocked by Grace's news this morning, but this is beyond anything I was expecting, at least so soon."

Winston smiled. "I'll give you some time to mull it over, of course. But I would like your answer as soon as possible."

"Of course, Winston. I'll get back to you very soon."

Winston stood and shook Elliot's hand. "I look forward to hearing from you."

"Thank you, sir… uh… Winston. I really appreciate this," he said as he left the office, practically walking on air.

As ELLIOT left Winston's office, Grace walked to Bradley's cubicle. "Good morning, Bradley."

Bradley stood up and smiled. "Good morning, Grace."

LET'S CHEAT! | 65

"I wonder if you have time to come to my office for a few minutes."

"Of course," he replied and followed her.

As soon as they were in her office with the door closed, Grace sat down behind her desk and carefully watched Bradley, wanting to catch his reactions to what she would say.

"Bradley, I've had my eye on you since you joined our firm. I admire and appreciate your talent and your potential here. I'm going to come directly to the point. I want you to come with me to Los Angeles and help me establish the new branch."

The shock was evident on Bradley's face. "You want me to go West with you?"

"I realize you have your husband, Matt, to consider, but to sweeten the pot and to entice you a bit, I'm going to make you a promise. How would you like to be a senior partner within just a few years after we've established our office in Los Angeles?"

Bradley stared at Grace as though he wasn't sure what she had just said. "That's a wonderful opportunity, Grace. I appreciate your confidence in me."

Grace smiled. "Yes. I'm hopeful that you'll be a big help in our new office. Eventually you'd have a crucial voice in establishing policy."

"I'm at a loss for words, Grace. Of course I'd like to do that. But you said it yourself. I have Matt to consider. I don't know if he would want to move to California, and there is also his position at the college. He's an associate professor, and he'd have to have a similar position somewhere in the Los Angeles area. I have no idea how difficult that might be."

"I can assure you that I will do everything in my power to help find a suitable teaching position for Matthew, but you're right. You must discuss all this with him."

Bradley beamed at Grace. "I can't tell you what an honor this is—"

"Okay, Bradley," Grace interrupted and laughed. "You don't have to lay it on. I know you appreciate the opportunity, and I hope that you can take it."

She grew serious. "But I have to warn you about something. I can assure you that Winston Kirby is making a similar suggestion to your friend Elliot Lawson. If too many associates and partners want to stay in New York, I'm afraid that although Winston likes you well enough, you'd be on the list of those who might have to be let go if you elect to stay. We would try to find something at another firm in New York for you, but I can't promise...."

"I get it, Grace. I'll talk to Matt and get back to you as quickly as I can."

"Thank you, Bradley, and I hope that we get the chance to work together in Los Angeles."

Bradley stood and left the office. "Wow," he muttered. "Two bombshells in one morning. I've got some serious talking to do with Matt...."

MATT was gathering his notes and papers together to put into the new briefcase Bradley had bought for him. His first class of the day was over, and he was wondering whether he had made the story about the murder of England's King Edward II colorful enough. He certainly had tried to bring it to life for his students.

He smiled guiltily when he remembered their reactions. He had told them about the red-hot poker the killers had jammed up the king's rectum in his sleep and seared the life out of him, on the queen's orders. His description of the king's piteous and bloodcurdling screams had drained the blood from the faces of all but the heartiest of the class. He was almost ashamed of having unnerved them like that, but at least they hadn't slept through today's lecture. And they would certainly remember it.

Someone cleared a throat to get his attention. Matt looked up to see Derrick Andrews.

"Hello, Mr. Andrews. Is there something I can do for you?"

"You can just call me Derrick, Dr. Sharp. Can I call you Matt?"

Matt smiled gently. "Probably not, Derrick. Perhaps in a few years, or at least after you've graduated. Since you're a student in one of my classes, that wouldn't really be appropriate."

Derrick just grinned back at him. "It was worth a try."

"Was there something specific...?"

"I just wanted to tell you how much I enjoyed your lecture today, Dr. Sharp."

Matt stared at Derrick curiously.

"Okay, *enjoyed* is not exactly the right word. I was *fascinated* by the horrible story you told us."

Matt was growing amused and just looked at Derrick.

"That didn't come out right. I didn't mean to say you were a horrible lecturer. I was just trying to say—"

"Okay, Derrick," Matt interrupted. "I think I understand what you were trying to say, and yes, the story of King Edward's death is truly horrifying. I am pretty sure there was a compliment in there somewhere?"

Derrick laughed. "Yes, there was. You made it seem so very real that my skin crawled."

"Thank you." Matt smiled again. "Now, was there something else?"

Derrick hesitated and looked down. "Yes, Dr. Sharp. I think you are *really* cute, and that guy with you in the library that time in the reading room is really lucky to have you." He blushed a dark red. "I'm gay too, Dr. Sharp, and I just wanted to tell you that if I were a little older and out of school, I would like to go out with you."

Matt thought carefully before he spoke. "You've given me a really nice compliment, Derrick, and I thank you again. But you said it yourself. I'm too *old* for you. And you *are* a student. I'm flattered by your attention, but we have nowhere to go with this. Don't you agree?"

Derrick sighed. "I know. But I just had to tell you, and I'm glad that I did. By the way, that husband of yours is a knockout too."

"See you in class next time, Derrick," Matt replied.

"Dr. Sharp, I have a really handsome older brother who's also gay and—"

"Goodbye, Derrick," Matt said with a chuckle as he picked up his briefcase and started to walk out of the classroom.

He was interrupted by a man stepping into the doorway to block his exit.

"Excuse me," Matt said, without looking closely at the man. "I'll just get out of your way—"

"Just a minute, Dr. Sharp. I want to talk to you."

Matt looked into the man's face and recognition registered as the man's name came to him. "Winthrop? Aren't you Gerald Winthrop?"

The man looked at Matt scornfully and made a dour face. "So you remember me? I'm a little surprised."

"Well, you were in my class just last spring semester. How can I help you?"

"I'll tell you. You can contact the dean's office and change my grade in your class."

Matt frowned. "Now why would I want to do that? As I recall, you at least passed the course."

"Just barely. That low grade you gave me did a real number on my overall grade point average. My GPA was 3.7 before you ruined it."

"Back up a minute, Gerald. I don't *give* grades to anyone. I *assign* grades that the student earns. To be brutally honest, you were lucky to receive a passing grade at all after that term paper you turned in at the end of the semester."

"You just *had it in for me*—all semester long, Dr. Sharp."

Matt glanced at the wall clock. "Look, Gerald. Another class will start coming in here any minute now. Let's go to my office if you want to discuss this further."

Gerald frowned. "No. I've got another class right now too. But I think you'd better think hard about changing my grade. My father has some clout around this place... things could tank for you, if you know what I mean."

"Threats aren't going to help you in the least, Gerald. Now you'll have to excuse me." Matt pushed his way past Gerald and started down the hall toward his office.

BRADLEY and Elliot sat at a booth in their favorite diner, Midtown Restaurant on East 55th Street.

"I don't know why I bother to look at this menu," Elliot remarked. "It doesn't change very often. I usually order the London broil sandwich whenever we come here, but I think I'll just get a burger this time."

Bradley mused, "And I guess I'm going to order the chicken salad platter."

After they placed their orders, they sat quietly for a few moments—deep in thought.

This California office thing is really going to be a huge problem. Matt isn't going to want to leave New York, and not just because of his job at the college. New York is home for him—and us. I don't want to go either, for that matter. Hell, we never even discussed living anywhere but here. I can almost hear Matt exploding already. This better not wreck our marriage!

"Excuse me," Elliot interrupted Bradley's thoughts. "Earth to Bradley—are you in there somewhere?"

Bradley blinked and grinned. "Sorry. I was just thinking about Matt." He looked at Elliot and wondered if he should reveal his big news about moving to the West coast.

Before he could begin, Elliot spoke up. "I've been waiting for lunch so we could get out of the office and talk. I have to tell you something."

"Funny you should say that," Bradley added. "I had the same idea. There's something I need to tell you too."

"So who goes first?" Elliot asked. "Want me to tell my news?"

He was interrupted by the waitress's arrival with two glasses of ice water.

Bradley thought for a moment. "Okay, Elliot, you go ahead. I'm all ears. Have you been thinking about moving to California?"

Elliot looked down at his hands on the table. "Well, you brought up the right subject, but that's not what I had in mind at all. I'm pretty sure I'm going to stay in New York."

"I *knew* you were going to say that," Bradley said.

"How would you know that?" Elliot insisted. "I didn't even know it myself until late this morning."

"Grace suggested that you would. We had a talk this morning. That was what I wanted to talk to you about."

"What? How would Grace know?"

Bradley looked directly at Elliot. "Because she knew Winston Kirby was going to ask you to stay here with him."

Elliot blinked. "And she told you this today?"

"Yes. It was when she asked me to move with her to Los Angeles."

"Wow. You knew my news even before I could tell you. That kind of takes the surprise off the table, so to speak."

"Yeah. But didn't Winston tell you that Grace was probably asking me the same kind of thing?" Bradley asked.

"He didn't say a word about it. And it's not like Grace and Winston to keep secrets from each other. He must have known and just didn't mention it."

"I guess so," Bradley said. "It sounds like they're making lists of who goes, or stays, where. Don't act so surprised—you know those two discuss pretty much everything. But back to the subject—are you going to take his offer?"

"Sure. I didn't really want to leave the city anyway. But are you really going to go to California? Surely you haven't decided something like that without talking to Matt first. Does he even know about any of this?"

Bradley sighed and thought about how Matt might look when he dropped the news on him. "No. I haven't had a chance to talk to him. I couldn't exactly call him on the phone to tell him anything like that."

"I suppose not. But why would you want to go to Los Angeles anyway? I didn't think you were especially crazy about it. I've always pictured you as a real New Yorker."

Bradley glanced at Elliot, trying to decide whether to tell him the rest of it. "I almost have to go, Elliot. Grace said if I stayed and too many others wanted to stay too, Winston would probably let me go."

"Wow. You really think so? I thought Winston liked you."

"I think he does. He just likes you better. And that's okay. I don't mind. I really think I might like the adventure of going West and helping start a new firm. Besides, I'd eventually get a senior partnership like you will pretty soon too. Matt's situation is the really big obstacle."

"You mean because it's the middle of the school term and he can't leave?"

"That's only one issue. It's much more complicated than that."

The arrival of their orders interrupted their discussion again.

"Well, I guess there's nothing more to be said until I can talk to Matt and see what he thinks," Bradley said with another sigh. "I really dread having to tell him about all this. I know he's not going to like it much."

Elliot nodded, and they began to eat their lunches.

"I'M GLAD you're back," Matt said to Clarice, who was sitting next to him on the sofa in his apartment. "It's been kind of lonely around here without you."

Clarice rolled her eyes and took another sip from her beer bottle. "Yes, I'm sure Bradley could hardly comfort you as you two rolled around on your bed doing carnal acts that I don't even want to hear about. Well, *maybe I do.*" She giggled.

Matt smirked. "I told you already about our scary trip to that leather bar over Thanksgiving. Wasn't that exciting enough for you?"

"Did Bradley *really* wet his pants?"

"Honest to God he really did. He let me put my hand on his wet crotch to prove it. So unless he spilled some beer on himself, he did it."

Clarice couldn't stop laughing. She had to put her beer bottle on the coffee table to keep from spilling it.

Matt chuckled a little, but he quickly stopped and pretended to be serious. "Wait a minute. I'm *not* going to laugh with you about this because I nearly did the same thing myself. And besides, it was a truly frightening experience. We both thought those guys were going to carve us up like the turkeys we really were for pulling such a dumb stunt in the first place."

Clarice stopped laughing. "You're right. And I have to agree with you. I'm actually surprised Bradley could think up such a thing. I'm even more shocked that you went along with it."

Matt sighed. "I know. It's even hard for *me* to believe when I think about it. Bradley and I aren't teenagers, after all."

"Even though you were acting like it," Clarice added in a low voice.

Nodding, Matt silently agreed. Then he remembered Clarice's reason for going west. "How's your mother doing? I meant to ask when you first got here."

"She's doing really well." Clarice smiled. "I can't tell you how relieved we all are that her recovery has been so smooth."

"That's terrific, Clarice. I'm so glad to hear it—"

At that moment the front door opened and Bradley walked into the apartment.

"Hi, lover," Matt called out. "Look who's back."

"Hey, Clarice. Nice to see you home again." He walked over and gave Matt a quick kiss and planted another one on Clarice's forehead. "If you two don't mind, I'm going to change out of these work clothes. I won't be long."

Matt grinned cheekily. "Need some help with that? It would be my pleasure."

Bradley managed a thin smile. "I appreciate it, sweetie, but if you did that we wouldn't be back for nearly an hour, and Clarice would get bored waiting for us."

"Bradley, if you'll tell me what size you wear, I'll get you a whole case of *Depends* for Christmas," Clarice said, laughing loudly

The stony look on Bradley's face quickly stopped her laughter.

"I'm sorry, Bradley. That was a cheap shot about a sore subject, and I promise it won't happen again," Clarice said.

"Thanks," Bradley said. "Obviously Matt told you the story even though I think we'd both like to forget about it. But don't worry—I'm not angry he spilled the beans. I figured he wouldn't be able to keep it a secret from you anyway. I'll be back shortly." He picked up his briefcase and headed for the bedroom.

"I shouldn't have said that," Clarice admitted. "When will I learn to keep my big mouth shut?"

"Oh, he's not really put out," Matt assured her. "But he does seem a little strained or tired today. Usually his sense of humor just pops out. I guess he's been really busy at work."

"I'm sure you're right. Listen, Matt, I think I'll just run along home and unpack. I'm a little tired too from the long flight so I'll see you two later. Tell Bradley how really sorry I am for that stupid remark."

Matt gave her a hug when she rose to leave, and then he followed her to the door. "I'll do it, Clarice. Don't worry—he still loves you. And again, I'm so glad that your mom is better and that you're back. We'll see you soon." He closed the door behind her and looked toward the bedroom, wondering whether or not he should join Bradley.

Instead, he sat back down on the sofa and picked up his beer.

"Where's Little Mary Sunshine?" Bradley asked when he returned a few minutes later, now dressed in shorts and a T-shirt.

"She had to go home and unpack. When she came over, she had just gotten back from the airport. I think she's pretty tired. Speaking of that, you look kind of whipped yourself. Are you okay, sweetheart?"

Bradley frowned. "I guess I'm all right, but I have to talk to you about something serious."

Matt's pulse quickened. "Is something wrong, Bradley? You really don't look very well. I noticed it the minute you came through the door."

"Something happened at the office today, and I've been worried about it all day."

Now Matt was becoming somewhat alarmed. "Bradley, tell me what happened. Don't keep me in suspense like this. You're scaring me."

"I guess I'd better not delay the news. I'll just tell you. Grace is expanding the firm. She's opening a branch in Los Angeles and she wants me to go with her."

Matt was so surprised that he said nothing for a moment. Bradley went on to tell him the rest of the details about the firm's split, including the eventual offer for senior partnerships someday in the future that he and Elliot had received.

At last Matt seemed to grasp the situation. "You really might get laid off if you don't agree to go with Grace? That doesn't seem very fair after all your hard work."

"I don't think it's personal on Winston's part. He just really wants to keep Elliot and he offered Elliot a pretty good incentive. If the numbers work out, it's possible I could stay on in New York too, but that's a big *if*."

"I know you're thinking about your own incentive too," Matt added.

"Well, a person doesn't get the chance for an important partnership like that every day. I might not ever get one under Winston, even if I managed to keep my job...."

Matt smiled suddenly. "What about moving to another firm in New York? There are lots of opportunities and so many other firms in the city."

"That's a possibility, of course. But I'd have to start all over again at a new firm. Who knows how long it would take me to get back to the level I've reached so far?"

This time Matt's face fell. "You really want to take this new job, don't you?"

Bradley frowned. "It's not that I really want to go to California. That's *nothing* to me. But the promise of a future partnership is a big deal, Matt."

"I know. I know. But you know the result of all this. If you go West, *I can't go with you.*" Matt's eyes filled with tears. "It's the middle of the school year, and I can't possibly leave with you in late winter."

Bradley put his arms around Matt and kissed his cheek. "I am aware of that, but it wouldn't be too long before the spring term ended. Then you could come join me in Los Angeles."

Matt's tear-filled eyes looked down. "Bradley, have you thought about my job at all?"

"What do you mean, sweetheart? Of course I have."

"Have you? I'm an associate professor on the road to a full professorship at the college. I've worked very hard trying to earn tenure and that professorship. It's just like you in your job. You want a partnership, and I want my own advancement."

"I know that you do."

"But you're not getting the *point*, Bradley. Asking me to leave is like asking you to quit your firm. We've both worked hard to get where we are. If I leave, then I have to start all over again in California. Oh I suppose I could take a sabbatical... or work on a book out there... maybe even try to get a position as a visiting professor. But there are lots of 'ifs' in there and not a lot of time to plan for any of this. It means a lot of unexpected hard work."

The reality of what Matt was saying finally hit Bradley. "You'd really have a tough time of it... this late in the year, wouldn't you?"

"Of course I could go, but I might not be able to make all the arrangements in time to leave next summer or even in the fall. I just don't know. This is all so unexpected. It's beginning to look like one of us loses—or both of us lose if I have to stay or can't swing it—very quickly. The result of that might be *we'd split up*." Matt began to cry hopelessly in Bradley's arms.

"Damn," Bradley muttered as he tried to soothe Matt. "I hadn't thought of all of this. But we *can't* split up. We're *married*."

Matt looked up at Bradley through his tears. "Do you really think we can stay married and live at opposite ends of the country?" he asked wearily. "Even for a short while would be difficult."

Bradley hugged him tighter. "Well, we're not going to just *give up*. We'll wait and see what the numbers look like when Grace gets the preferences from the staff. Maybe there's a way that I can stay. I'll talk to Grace again and tell her all of our concerns. She likes me. She'll think of something. I can have a little talk with Winston too."

"I hope you're right, Bradley," Matt replied. "We've been through too much to just lose our relationship this way."

"I know, sweetheart. We've just got to keep positive and see how it all plays out. Would you like to go out for dinner tonight?"

Matt shook his head. "I'm not hungry. This has just blown me away—"

Bradley put his arms around Matt and held him close.

Chapter
EIGHT

GRACE made it out of the elevator but not to her office. If the receptionist had not seen her fall, the doctors said later, the heart attack would have killed her. But fortunately for Grace, the receptionist Mrs. Barnes *did* see the fall and quickly called 911.

Now in a hospital bed in a premier facility, Grace lay quietly listening to the soothing voice of Winston Kirby.

"There's nothing to discuss, Grace, and you know it." He looked at her unmoving form resting under crisp white sheets. "And I'm really pleased that you're taking it all so well."

"I may be hardheaded and tough in the courtroom, Winston, but I'm not *stupid*," Grace replied softly. "I realize that I can't go to California now to open a new office. And yes, I know that I'm going to have to take it easy for a while. But I think there *is* something to discuss."

Winston smiled warmly. "You mean like what kind of flowers you'd like for me to bring you while you recuperate?" He chuckled at his shallow wit and looked around at the garden of arrangements that already threatened to fill the room.

"I like red roses," Grace replied with an answering smile, "but what I meant was the new office plans. I think you should simply take my place and head out to the sunny coast yourself."

"What? *Me*? I was sure we'd have to drop the whole idea."

Now it was Grace's turn to chuckle. "Now, Winston, you know very well that you could be just as effective in setting up that branch out there as I could. Maybe you'd be even better at it because you would have a fresh approach."

"I'd like to point out that you set up the original firm here in New York, and you have the experience in that area which I lack."

"Winston, you underestimate yourself. I picked you to head the New York office when I thought I was leaving. I have every confidence that you can create the new one. You'll be taking half of our partners and associates, after all, and you'll all work very well together. I have no doubt about it in the least."

He appeared unconvinced so she quietly looked him directly in the eye. "Once you get there, I just *know* you'll love California." She saw the look of doubt that crossed his face.

"Besides, Winston, you wouldn't want to *jeopardize* my recovery," she added coyly. "I would rest ever so much more easily with the knowledge that you're *saving me* by taking the project over." Grace could tell now that she had turned the tide of battle against Winston by his defeated air. But she refrained from gloating and remained patient while playing her role.

He shook his head slowly at her. "Now, Grace, you know you're not playing fair by manipulating me this way. I'm beginning to see what it would be like to face you at the opposite table in court."

She smiled. "Of course I'm not, Winston, but you know what they say—life isn't fair." After a pause she added, "What if I offered a little extra incentive?"

His eyes narrowed a little and he asked curiously, "And whatever did you have in mind to tempt me?"

She smiled broadly. "I'll bet that in the depths of your heart you really wanted to head up the California office all the time, and you just didn't tell me because you thought that I wanted it so badly."

Winston laughed. "I see that your *imagination* has not been dimmed by a hospital stay."

"Ah, my dear friend, Winston. Sparring with you has helped me feel better already." Now Grace sat up and smiled. She could tell that she was going to prevail in this. She could cajole or finesse him and thus win him over, and she knew it.

"All right, Grace. I give up. I'll be a good sport and do this just for you. But I wouldn't move to California for anyone else but you." And he added sincerely, "This is going to require some fast talking and heavy persuasion to convince my wife."

"If it would help, have her come to visit me, and I'll help soften the blow."

He looked out the window and said, "I will probably have to take you up on that."

"Now about that incentive I promised. Perhaps a name change to McKenna, Kirby, and Associates would suit you?"

Winston smiled. "You really mean that, Grace?"

She nodded and smiled back warmly.

"I have to admit that *does* have a really nice ring to it."

"I thought you might like that. Besides, fair is fair. And you are making a big and certainly unexpected sacrifice by doing this, despite any reward that I could give you."

"It's a generous offer, and I gratefully accept. However, let's not tire you out any further. We can go over the necessary details after you have more time to recover. I'll take my leave now, and you get some rest."

"Thank you, Winston," she replied tiredly.

"And thank you, Grace. You won't regret it. I'll do my very best to make us all successful—"

At last Grace's eyes began drooping from fatigue, so he crept out of the room and pulled the door closed quietly.

RATHER than call a meeting to address the ramifications of Grace's heart attack, Winston simply issued a printed notice to all the staff.

> *As all of you are now aware, Grace McKenna suffered a mild heart attack in our offices on Wednesday morning. Thankfully, she is recovering nicely and resting comfortably at New York Presbyterian Hospital. It is too soon for her to receive visitors just yet, but I know that she would appreciate any cards or notes and certainly your prayers. In lieu of flowers, Grace asked that if you desire to acknowledge her, send a contribution to your favorite charity.*

This sudden emergency has necessitated a change in our plans for expansion to the West Coast. Grace will now remain with the New York office, and I will be taking charge of establishing our new branch office in Los Angeles. If this changes any of your plans for the division of our firm, please notify me in writing, and we will sort out who moves to California and who remains in New York. Thank you for your patience and understanding as we move forward with our creation of two firms from the resources of what is now McKenna, Kirby, and Associates.

—Winston Kirby
West Coast Branch of McKenna, Kirby, and Associates

"THIS business at Bradley's office, Clarice," Matt moaned. "It's been a mess. I feel like I've been on a rollercoaster for the past week. I wonder what will happen next."

"Poor Matt," Clarice replied sympathetically. She reached across from her chair in Matt's living room and patted his arm as he sat on the sofa. "Now maybe Bradley won't have to leave after all. I wouldn't think his boss is in any condition to go anywhere and start up a new business."

Matt nodded. "That's pretty much what I think too. Don't get me wrong—I wouldn't wish anything awful like that to happen to his boss, but it's our whole future we're talking about."

Clarice patted his arm again. "Of course you wouldn't, sweetie. Things just happen."

"A lot's happened all right," Matt said and frowned.

A cell phone rang, and both Matt and Clarice grabbed their phones at the same time.

"It's mine," Clarice announced and then spoke softly to her caller in a very brief conversation. "I have to go," she said. "That was my cousin, and I need to call her back"

"Anything wrong?"

"No. We just need to visit a little about Mother. I'll call you later."

As Clarice opened the door to go, she saw that Bradley stood there, key in hand ready to unlock it.

"Thanks, Clarice," he said with a grin. "How did you know I was here?"

"I'm psychic," she exclaimed and kissed him on the cheek. "Sorry, but I've got to go." She waved to Matt as she hurried on her way.

Bradley closed the door and smiled. "I've always had that effect on women."

"I know better than that," Matt replied. "You're a hunk, and you know it. You wouldn't be single if you were straight."

"I'm not *single* as a gay man either." He walked over and gave Matt a lingering kiss.

"You're awfully chipper today. What's going on?"

Bradley reached into his coat pocket and pulled out a sheet of paper. "Take a look at this. There always seem to be surprises at work these days."

Matt took the paper and read Winston Kirby's announcement.

"Wow. I see what you mean. So Grace is staying in New York, and Kirby becomes an equal partner with her. That sounds like really great news for us, sweetheart. Now you won't have to move. That will really save us a lot of trouble."

"That's the way it looks to me too." He kissed Matt again. "Want to go to the bedroom and celebrate?"

"There's nothing I'd like better," Matt agreed as they got up and headed in that direction.

Chapter **NINE**

BRADLEY was working in his office when Grace called.

"Grace, how nice to hear from you. Winston told everyone at the office you were able to have visitors so I was planning to drop by this afternoon, if that's all right with you."

Grace cleared her throat. "What a coincidence, Bradley. I was just calling to ask if you could visit me today. There's something I'd really like to discuss with you."

"This is perfect timing. By the way, you sound just *wonderful*. Are you doing as well as you sound?"

"Well, I'll be even better when I get out of this hospital, and the doctors say I'm doing remarkably well. But I won't keep you from your work, especially since this is on my dime, so to speak," she said, chuckling softly. "I'll see you later today."

Bradley hung up and sat for a moment, mulling over the call. *I wonder if she's going to confirm that I get to stay in New York. Surely that's it. Perhaps she's got something in mind for me to do for her here in the office. I guess I'll find out soon enough.*

The afternoon fairly flew by after Bradley returned from a quick lunch with Elliot. It was no surprise that Elliot had told him he was headed for California with Winston Kirby. In Bradley's opinion, Elliot was fortunate to have no real commitments here in New York that would be disturbed by his move to the West Coast.

Bradley knocked gently on Grace's door and waited for her invitation to enter.

"Hi there, boss," he said with a ready smile. "I guess you're the real rose in the middle of this flower garden," he added, gesturing to the many blossoms crowding the room.

"You're ever the gentleman, Bradley. If I were a cynic, I might doubt your sincerity. But I know you too well." She smiled and pointed to a chair next to her bed.

Bradley smiled back. "You really do look great. I'll bet you won't be here much longer."

"You're quite right. The doctors say I can go home tomorrow or the next day, depending on a few more tests."

"That's great news. But I hope you won't try to come back to the office too quickly," Bradley cautioned. "There's no point in your ending up back here again. You probably need to rest a little more at home first."

Grace frowned. "Right again, Bradley. They say I should stay home for at least another week and then only come back for half-days. I can just imagine all the partying that goes on at the office while I'm gone." She laughed gently.

"Don't forget that Winston is still in the office. He keeps us all in line, and he makes sure things keep moving along smoothly."

"Now that you mention Winston Kirby, he's exactly the person I wanted to visit with you about when I called this morning."

"You want to talk to me about Winston? That's kind of a surprise."

"Then I'll back up and begin again," Grace replied. "I'm sure you know that I'll not be going to Los Angeles to open our new branch. I read Winston's memo so I'm aware of what the staff has been told."

Bradley beamed with pleasure for a moment. "I'm not pleased about what happened to *you*, Grace, but I *am* really happy you're staying in New York. I want you to know that I think of you as a friend as well as my boss. You've been so supportive since you brought me into the firm."

"I hope I was smart enough to spot great potential. And it's been fun knowing you and Matt—even helping you celebrate a few anniversaries over the years."

"That's why I feel close enough to you to tell you that Matt and I have been terribly stressed out because it began to look like we might have some serious problems in our marriage as well as in our business lives because of this California move."

Now Grace frowned again. "I was afraid you'd think I called you to say I wanted you to stay here in New York."

Bradley looked puzzled. "You mean that's not the case?"

"Well, it is and it isn't."

"That's a little ambiguous, isn't it? What do you mean?"

"Bradley, it's true that I would like for you to stay here— eventually."

Now it was Bradley's turn to frown. "This isn't sounding the way I'd hoped, Grace. Just go ahead and tell me what you have in mind."

"You're right," Grace agreed. "I'm drawing this out and holding you in suspense. Here's the gist of it all. I'd like for you to remain in New York *after* you go to Los Angeles with Winston for a few months."

"What? You want me to go West just for a few months? Why?"

Grace gave Bradley a serious look. "This is between the two of us, Bradley. I mean that most sincerely. I want you to go with Winston and his team as *my representative*. I intend to make sure that my interests are respected and protected when this new branch opens."

Bradley's mouth was partially open from surprise. "Are you saying that you *don't trust* Winston? Why would you make him a full partner, then?"

"Perhaps I put all of this too strongly," Grace backtracked. "I didn't mean to imply any distrust in him at all," she insisted. "I'm sure he will be brilliant with the tasks ahead. I just meant that I want you to advise him from the point of view I would take if I were there."

Bradley shook his head slightly. "I doubt he's going to take kindly to any advice I would offer. He's a full partner, and I'm just a junior partner."

"Not exactly. As of today I'm appointing you my personal representative in the California office—and I mean *immediately*."

Bradley's eyes opened wide in surprise. Before he could help himself, he jumped up, clapped his hands, cheered, and rushed to plant a kiss on Grace's cheek. "Thank you," he gushed. "It means a great deal to me that you trust me that much."

Grace rolled her eyes and grinned. "I appreciate how happy you are, Bradley, but please sit down so I can finish what I want to say."

Bradley calmed himself and sat back down. "Sorry, Grace. I guess I got a little carried away for a minute."

She smiled and softened her tone. "Now don't worry about Winston. I'm having a little chat with him later today. I'll explain this to him in such a diplomatic way that he'll cheerfully accept you in this new position. I might even be able to make him think that it's *his idea*. Besides, despite what I told you earlier, I've come to believe that he likes and respects you more than I thought he did. It will work out very well, believe me. Just remember that you'll report directly to me. You won't be under his authority."

Bradley frowned again. "It would be just for a few months? You promise?"

Grace laughed. "Do you want me to cross my heart like a little kid and say *hope to die?*"

"Of course not," Bradley began. "*Well, maybe.*" He laughed.

"Here goes," Grace said, crossing her heart with an *X* and then adding, "And I hope—"

"No. Don't go that far with it, Grace. Remember we're in a hospital room. It would be unlucky if you said the rest."

"I had no idea you were so superstitious."

"I'm not. I just don't want you to say it. Anyway, I'm going to need some luck when I have to explain to Matt that I'm going to LA after all. He's not going to be pleased. And I'll miss him."

"I have a thought," Grace said with a gleam in her eye. "Why don't you go home and come back here about seven tonight *with Matt*. I'll explain this to him personally. Perhaps that will help soften the blow, at least a little."

Bradley thought it over for a moment. "Hmmm. That might really help, Grace. Are you sure that you wouldn't mind?"

"Bradley, I'm the one who's causing a lot of inconvenience to you both. Let me share some of the blame that's going to fall on you for working for me in the first place."

"Okay. You talked me into it. Thanks so much, Grace. You said about seven tonight?"

"Yes. That should give Winston and me a chance to have our little discussion and get things arranged for you to accompany him west."

"Good. Well, I'll see you this evening."

Bradley quickly left the room and headed down the hallway. "All right, Matt," Bradley said to himself as he approached the elevator. "You've just got to understand that this *has to be done*. I'll make it up to you somehow—"

MATT and Bradley were sitting in the back of a taxi on their way home from Presbyterian Hospital later that night. Both were tired and a little on edge.

"Okay, she's not around. What do you *really* think, sweetheart?" Bradley asked cautiously.

Matt was silent.

"Sweetheart? Matt?"

"I'm thinking about this. The whole thing catches me a little off guard. I was sure you'd stay in New York. Now you're going to Los Angeles after all."

"But you heard what Grace said. It's only for about three months. I'll be home even before the end of your spring term."

"Bradley, I thought you were a good attorney."

"What exactly does *that* mean?"

"That means that you should be able to read between the lines."

"Huh? What are you getting at, sweetheart?"

Matt looked miserable. "I mean that she says *now* that she wants her point of view represented at the beginning, but I bet she'll ask you later to stay on and represent her *indefinitely* in the new branch office."

"Do you actually think Grace would do something like that? You're letting your imagination run away with you."

"Well, maybe it hasn't occurred to her just yet, but what if it did later? You'll already be there in place."

"That's an awfully big assumption based on nothing, Matt. Do you really believe that?"

"I guess I don't really. But if it did happen that way, Bradley...."

"Let's calm down, Matt. Grace would never do anything to hurt the two of us. Deep down you know that's true. Am I right?" He put his arms around Matt and kissed him lightly.

Matt hesitated. "Oh, I guess that's so."

"Then let's not jump to conclusions. We'll assume that I'll only be gone for three months and let it go at that. You'll notice that she didn't hand me a book on what to study to pass the bar exam in California. That's a good sign my California trek will be short and she wants me back in New York. In the meantime, we'll find ways to get together from time to time."

"How do you figure?" Matt pouted.

"I won't be gone until after Christmas and New Year's so we'll have those two holidays together. Then I'll fly home for a weekend here and there. You can fly out west during spring break and maybe for a weekend or two. It'll all pass by in a hurry, and we'll get some fun short vacations out of it."

"You make it sound like a series of holidays."

Bradley smiled, beginning to feel that things might work out well after all. "It will be, honey. I promise. We'll be separated for a little while, that's true. But we'll have lots of time together too. You'll see."

Matt brightened a little. "Maybe you're right. I guess I was looking at it in the worst possible light. I'll try to see it your way."

"I love you, sweetheart," Bradley assured him before kissing him again.

"And I love you too," Matt mumbled through a series of kisses. Then the cab reached their apartment building.

"We'll finish this upstairs," Bradley promised as he paid the cabbie and then slammed the taxi door.

MATT sat at the desk in his office, leaned back, and took a deep breath as he stared for a moment at the computer screen. He had just entered the last of the fall semester grades for his students and sent the official forms to the dean's office. At last he could relax and prepare to enjoy being away from campus for a few weeks. It would be particularly important this time since Bradley would be leaving for the West coast before very long.

A knock sounded on the door. "Come in. It's open."

The door slowly opened, and Gerald Winthrop stood in the doorway. He glared at Matt and stepped into the office. "I've come for a talk, Dr. Sharp."

Matt tried to erase the surprise on his face. "Sit down, Gerald," he said, pointing to the small sofa in front of his desk.

Gerald unbuttoned his heavy coat, but he didn't take it off. He shrugged and sat down. "I won't stay very long. I guess you're finishing your grades."

"No. They're complete and already sent. How can I help you, Gerald?"

"I already told you. Change my grade. I need to graduate with honors next spring."

Matt frowned. "I've explained to you that I'm not going to do that."

"You mean you haven't even been thinking about it? It could cause you a lot of trouble if you don't."

"Gerald, aren't you smart enough to know you shouldn't threaten a professor. That's the last thing you should do. Suppose I get a form from a prospective employer someday who wants me to write an evaluation of you. What kind of comments do you think I would write?"

"I'll never list you as a reference anyway."

"Your transcript will list all your courses, and it wouldn't be difficult for a company recruiter or executive to find out the names of your instructors and professors. Sometimes they contact all of them— particularly for junior and senior course work. "

"You're beating around the bush, Dr. Sharp. Just raise my grade, and I'll never bother you again."

"Gerald, you got a low grade because you were lazy and put very little effort into your work."

"What's that supposed to mean?"

"I don't know why I need to tell you. You're the one who googled the information on your term paper subject and practically copied the information from Wikipedia articles online. You barely changed the words to hide what you were doing. Did you really think that professors aren't aware of Wikipedia? I always read articles that apply to my students' topics on papers. We're not stupid, Gerald."

Gerald blushed a dark red. "What are you complaining about? It's research, isn't it?"

"It's the closest thing to plagiarism I can think of, short of flat-out copying someone else's work. In some places you *did* just about copy the articles almost word for word. You're lucky I didn't contact the dean and recommend your expulsion for plagiarism. But at least you had the decency to rewrite some of it, which is why I gave you a *little* credit. That's the reason I *assigned* a passing grade to you. But you have some real talent, Gerald. You could have done a really great job on your paper. I got the feeling you waited until a couple of days before the paper was due to begin work on it."

Gerald stood up. "I had four other papers to write. I didn't have time to do the kind of research you mean."

"And look at what happened, Gerald."

"You're just mad at me because I didn't try to flirt with you in class, Dr. Sharp. We all know you're gay and that you *examine* the good-looking guys in class! It's almost like you're cruising for a quick fuck. I don't know how you knew that I'm gay, but you must have expected me to—"

"Now you've gone too far," Matt exploded as he jumped out of his chair. "My private life has nothing to do with you or any other student on this campus. I've never had any personal interest in any student, and it's outrageous for you to suggest... no, *accuse me* of that! Now I'm going to give you about five seconds to get out of my office before I call security. As it is, I'm certainly going to make a report to the dean before the holidays. Get out!"

Gerald trudged toward the door. "Okay. I'm going. But you haven't heard the last of me." He slammed the office door, leaving Matt red-faced and breathing hard through his anger. He picked up the phone on his desk and dialed the number for the dean's office.

Chapter
TEN

WHEN Matt got home, Bradley was already there sprawled out on the sofa asleep. At first Matt didn't notice him so he slammed the front door, still consumed with anger from the episode with Gerald Winthrop.

Startled, Bradley sat up and looked around. "Are we at war?" he asked.

Matt blinked in surprise. "Sorry, Bradley. I didn't see you over there. I was just too angry to think about you being here."

"Uh oh. Something tells me you had an *adventure* at school today. Want to tell me all about it?"

Matt sat down and allowed Bradley to cuddle up and hold him while he told his story. When he had finished recounting what had happened, Bradley tried to soothe him as much as possible.

"Sweetie, don't let him spoil your holidays or the time we have left together."

Matt sniffed and wiped a few tears.

"Sorry. I shouldn't have brought that last part up to remind you. Look, the semester is over. It's nearly Christmas. And that idiot can't really do anything to hurt you, can he?"

"No. I guess not. I went to the dean's office and made a report after Gerald left. The dean just asked if I had kept the student's term paper as evidence in case the student tried to file a complaint. There's no proof of any kind that I've ever harassed a student at any time. The dean thinks it's just a matter of Gerald blowing off steam in his frustration."

"Well, it sounds like there's nothing to worry about."

"I guess so. Gerald just made me so damned furious. No one has ever suggested such a thing before and—"

"And it won't go anywhere either. I know it's hard, but you just need to try to forget it. I bet the kid will really be sorry later. I wouldn't be surprised if you get a sincere apology."

"That seems a little unlikely to me, but I hope you're right...."

"Now give me a nice kiss, and then you can go take a shower. We'll have a cozy evening at home and start thinking of ways to get together during those three months that I'll be in California."

"Okay. You're right. I'll try not to let Gerald spoil our holidays."

"That's the spirit. Off to the shower with you. Maybe I'll surprise you and join in."

Matt smiled for the first time. "I'll be waiting for you. Thanks for making me feel better, Bradley."

"That's what I'm here for...."

TENTATIVELY at first, the handsome blond man skated onto the ice until he reached a wall where he could stop and look up and around. The view from the ice was dazzling. The blinking, glittering Christmas tree at Rockefeller Center with its thousands of colored lights was only part of the glamour of the scene.

Flashing white oversize snowflakes lit up a whole building, an enormous gold statue sparkled with water flowing into the fountain, and huge white angels with golden horns glowed in the night along the walkways filled with tourists and even some real New Yorkers. He smiled as he noted all the camera phones and digital cameras the tourists used to take it all home to share. Every time he saw this spectacular scene at Christmas, he was filled with awe.

Trying to get into his rhythm, the skater carefully began his first circle around the rink, making sure not to go too fast or to bump into someone. *I should skate more than just once a year, and I might get a whole lot better at this.*

After a few turns around the rink, the blond man found himself skating to the beat of the Christmas music blaring cheerfully all around him. Filled with confidence now, he spun around a corner a little too fast and crashed to the ice with a hard bump.

"Are you okay?" someone asked.

He looked up into the toothy white smile of a beautiful dark-haired man standing above him. Bradley grinned down at him and winked.

"Uh, I guess I was overdoing it," Matt replied, trying to stand up.

"Here, let me help you," the dark-eyed stranger insisted, offering his hand.

The blond man looked into green eyes that twinkled like Christmas lights. "Thanks, Bradley. Uh... I mean *stranger*. I guess I'd better be more careful."

Now the stranger offered his hand again, saying, "Hi. My name is Hans. What's yours?"

The blond looked at the stranger suspiciously this time. "*Hans*? Hans what? *Brinker*?"

"You guessed it," Hans replied, grinning from ear to ear.

"Hans Brinker? You've got to be kidding."

"Play the game, Matt. That's what you always tell me. Now what was your name? I don't believe you told me—"

"All right," the blond man snapped. "My name's Scrooge. Ebenezer Scrooge. Eb for short."

"Do tell? That's a mighty famous name. Do you live up to it?" Hans asked, smiling again.

"Well, there are some folks *who are going to find out come Christmas Day*," Eb replied with a crooked grin.

"Such Christmas spirit you have," Hans remarked. "Anyway, Eb, would you like to skate with me?"

Good spirits restored, Eb reached out to take hold of Hans's hands. "Sure. Why not?"

"White Christmas" began playing on the sound system. With their hands joined, Eb and Hans began skating to the music among the many other skaters now on the ice. After a few times around the rink, Hans put his arm around Eb so that they skated even more smoothly.

"This is fun," Eb remarked. "We could do this all night—"

"As enjoyable as that would be," Hans said, "I'm actually getting a little cold. What about going upstairs and having a cup of cocoa or something in one of the cafes?"

"That's a good idea. Then we could walk around and just look at all these wonderful lights everywhere."

Just as they were about to leave the ice together, a somewhat chunky girl with auburn curls sticking out from under her wool cap skated up to them.

"Excuse me," she called, a little breathlessly. "Don't I know you two from somewhere?"

Hans turned and looked at her a little coldly. "No, I don't think so."

"Well, I think she looks very familiar," Eb declared. "What's your name, honey?"

"Ethel Mertz," the girl declared with a sly smile at Bradley. "Like Lucy Ricardo's friend on *I Love Lucy*. I knew you'd like my name."

"Of course," Eb said. "I'd know you anywhere. Well, Hans Brinker and I were just about to go have a cup of hot chocolate. Would you like to join us?"

Hans frowned. "She doesn't look like she wants anything to drink."

Ethel just smiled and shook her head. "No thanks. You're very kind to offer, but I'm just here to enjoy the Christmas spirit on the ice. So long." She skated away into the crowd of other skaters.

Eb reached over and pinched Hans on the cheek. "*Play the game*, Bradley. She didn't come to spoil our moment. And she's gone already."

"*How* did she even know we were going to be here?" Hans asked. "I thought this was *our* date tonight."

"It *is* our date," Eb whispered back, "I told her we'd be here tonight. She thought skating sounded like fun, but she promised to stay out of our way. She just came over to say hello… and she's off skating somewhere by herself."

"Okay," Bradley said, his good humor restored. "It's just that we'll be separated soon, and I wanted to be alone with you on Christmas Eve."

A tear trickled down Eb's face. "You didn't have to *remind me*."

"Please don't cry. I'm sorry for being so cross. Shame on me. Here I just met such a wonderfully handsome, sweet man too, and I'm excited to spend some time with him in this really beautiful place."

"Well, let's go get that cup of hot chocolate you mentioned," Eb replied. "It's colder out here than I thought it would be."

CHRISTMAS morning came all too soon for Matt. It meant that Bradley would be gone that much more quickly. He awakened as soon as it started to get light through the bedroom window drapes. But he closed his eyes and snuggled even closer into Bradley's arms which already encircled him.

Bradley stirred and murmured something unintelligible. Then he grew still once more.

Despite wanting to stay wrapped up with Bradley, Matt felt the unmistakable call to visit the bathroom. And the call was becoming more and more insistent. No longer able to ignore it, he slipped gently out of bed and padded into the bathroom, hoping to let Bradley sleep.

Matt had an inspiration before returning to bed a few minutes later. He turned on the living room Christmas tree lights and plugged in the string of twinkling ones that ran around the mantle and down the sides of the fireplace. Instantly, the room glowed cozily with colored lights for when Bradley and he got up to open their presents. As a last touch, he flipped the switch to turn on the electric fireplace to give the room added warmth. Pleased with the effect, Matt crept back to the bedroom and snuggled with Bradley once more.

BRADLEY'S eyes popped open a few hours later. He saw by the bedside alarm clock that it was after nine. He turned to awaken Matt, but he found that Matt was already gone, and his side of the bed was no longer warm.

"Good morning, sugar," Matt greeted him when Bradley stumbled into the kitchen. "Can I pour you a cup of fresh coffee?"

"How long have you been up?" Bradley asked, rubbing his eyes. "I can't believe I slept so late."

"About fifteen or twenty minutes, I guess," Matt replied. "I let us both sleep longer since we had such a late evening at Rockefeller Center. Now about that coffee... and by the way, Merry Christmas."

Bradley smiled happily. "Merry Christmas back, sweetheart. Give me a Christmas kiss."

Matt finally broke away from the lengthy kiss and laughed. "You stopped in the bathroom to gargle after you got up. I'm impressed."

"I wanted our first Christmas Day kiss to be a sweet one," Bradley said with a sly grin. "Don't bother about my coffee. You have a seat, and I'll pour it myself. You already did your part by making a pot of it while I was still asleep."

"Want me to make us a little breakfast? Or would you rather try to find an open coffee shop?" Matt asked when they were both seated at the kitchen table.

"I have an idea," Bradley said. "How about I make us a brunch of waffles or pancakes or something like that in a couple of hours? I don't get the chance to cook much anymore and you know I can be pretty good at it. But let's open our gifts first."

Bradley took Matt's hand and started to lead him toward the brightly decorated living room.

"Sounds like a great plan to me." Matt stopped to pick up his mug. "Bring your coffee, and let's go see what Santa brought."

"Wow. You already turned on the lights. It looks great in here," Bradley exclaimed. "I just love Christmas lights and decorations."

"Me too. Shall I play Santa first?" Matt asked.

Bradley smiled mysteriously. "Let me go first, then you can take a turn."

Matt seated himself on the sofa and sipped his coffee. "I'm glad we decided not to buy a lot of presents this year. We both already have so much anyway."

"That's true," Bradley agreed as he searched under the tree for something. "We've got each other, and that's the most important thing."

"I have a confession to make," Matt said softly, looking down at his cup. "I've been meaning to tell you something for a while now, but I think I've finally gotten the courage."

Bradley stopped looking under the tree and turned to face him. "What's up, sweetie? You know you can tell me anything."

Matt looked away and hesitated. "Okay. Here goes. I've been seeing other men behind your back."

Startled for a moment, Bradley just stared at Matt, his mouth partially hanging open in surprise.

"You might as well know who they are," Matt admitted. "First there was Charles Dickens, and then Percy Plantagenet, followed by Dick Placid. I think he looked a lot like Zorro. Then there was Brad Pitt and some drug dealer I met in an S and M bar, and more recently this guy called Hans Brinker."

After the first name, Bradley caught on and was laughing out loud by the time Matt had finished his cheating list. "You really had me going there for a second," he said. "I should have known what you meant from the beginning."

Matt was laughing too. "We've had some really good times lately...." He stopped and grew serious. Then a tear rolled down his face.

"Oh, Matt," Bradley cried. "It's not the end of anything. We've *always* had good times together, and we're going to have a lot more too. Don't cry, baby."

Bradley came over to the sofa and sat down next to Matt so he could cradle him in his arms.

"I'm going to miss you *so much*," Matt murmured through his tears.

"Come on, honey. It's only for a little while, and we'll see each other from time to time on weekends and during spring break. Please don't cry anymore, or you'll make me cry too."

Matt's crying slowed down to a few sniffs. "You're right. And I shouldn't spoil Christmas morning."

"You're not spoiling anything, but you really *should* cheer up. I've got an idea. How about this summer when we're back together, we go on a special vacation to someplace really great? You be thinking about it, and so will I. Then we'll decide where this spring and make plans for the summer. How does that sound?"

Matt finally smiled. "That does sound like a good idea. It would give us something *big* to be looking forward to." He gave Bradley a lingering kiss. "I know I can always count on you to make something wonderful out of a bad situation."

"You mean like climbing out of a ladies' room window and running down an alley?"

Now Matt really laughed. "Something like that,"

"Now you sit here while I find a Christmas gift for you under the tree." He got up and resumed his search. At last he cried, "Here it is."

Matt looked at the small box. "It's not a very big package."

"You already get *a big package* every day as it is," Bradley announced while Matt laughed. "Aren't I enough for you in that department?"

"All right," Matt agreed. "That's very true, and I'm not complaining. Now let me open this *Christmas package*."

It was a small white box wrapped in red satiny paper with a white ribbon and bow. Matt carefully opened it and took out a gold disk about the size of a dollar coin. It had a slender gold chain attached to it, and there was an engraved infinity symbol on the front.

"It's beautiful," Matt exclaimed. "I love it."

"Look on the back," Bradley insisted.

In beautiful engraved script, the back of the disk read, *Bradley and Matt—together forever.*

"Oh, Bradley," Matt burst into tears again.

"Now wait a minute, sweetie. Stop crying and look under the cotton at the bottom."

Matt looked inside again, and a second disk and chain lay there. This one read, *Matt and Bradley—together forever.*

"Two?" Matt asked, and sniffed.

Bradley giggled. "Well, one's for me. You get the one with my name written first, and I get the other one. When we're apart, we can always look at the disks around our necks and have another reminder of our love and our marriage."

Fresh tears sprang up in Matt's eyes so Bradley had to take the disks and place each one around the appropriate neck. "Quit crying, and I'll get you some tissues to blow your nose."

"I love them, sweetheart. They're just as personal as our wedding rings."

"We can always look at our rings, of course, but the engraving is easier to read on the disks. And it's an extra reminder—right near your heart."

Bradley left to get the tissues while Matt held the little disk and smiled before giving it a little kiss.

"I love you, Bradley," Matt said when Bradley returned.

"I love you back, Dr. Sharp. Merry Christmas, and give us another kiss."

Chapter
ELEVEN

THE day before New Year's Eve, Bradley was stretched out full-length on the sofa watching TV while Matt put the luncheon dishes into the dishwasher.

On screen a blond man sat on a sofa in a trendy apartment. His companion was a beautiful brunette dressed in a sexy but disheveled outfit. She had her arms wrapped around the man as she kissed him fervently and ran her fingers through his hair.

"Oh, George! I just can't make myself leave you!" She kissed him again while George looked frantically at the wristwatch on his raised arm behind her back.

"Now Gina, your flight leaves in just an hour. You wouldn't want to miss it and your weekend with your mother, would you? She'd be so disappointed."

"You're right! I really can't do that. I promised her I'd come for a few days. I just hope she doesn't start in with nagging me again to get married."

George looked a little shocked. "So do I." The audience laughed. "Of course, I'd rather you stayed here all day so we could go back to bed and make love all—"

She put a finger over his lips and sat up abruptly. "Don't say another word, or I'll never leave! I've got to get out of here right now while I still can."

George looked apologetic. "Gosh, Gina. I'll count the seconds 'til you're back next weekend! Here's your bag." He whipped the bag out from behind the sofa. The audience laughed. "It was so clever of you to bring it with you last night...." He frowned slightly, and the audience laughed again.

"One last kiss," she begged.

"Of course." George grinned. Then he dipped her over like a dancer while planting the kiss on her she wanted. He lifted her back up, and smiled broadly as she visibly took a deep breath.

She seemed to collect her thoughts a moment before she finally grabbed the bag. Then she fled toward the front door of the apartment, looking back over her shoulder at George as she went. This caused her to bump into the door, and the audience laughed loudly this time.

She quickly recovered, blew George a kiss with her free hand, and scurried out, closing the door firmly behind her.

"Whew!" George took a deep breath. "That was too close!" he murmured as he looked again at this wristwatch and counted down, "One, two, and three...."

The doorbell rang. George smoothed his hair and his clothing before he flung the door open.

"Marjorie, sweetheart!" he called to the attractive blonde who rushed into the apartment, dropping her bag on the floor. "I've missed you so much! When you said you'd be free for the whole weekend, I packed a bag and here I am."

"Lucky me." He replied, and then kissed her. He broke from the kiss, turned to face the television camera, and winked. The audience laughed once more and clapped loudly.

The picture froze, and the program title appeared over the lovers in bright red-and-yellow letters, *Lucky in Love*. Music blared as noisy applause echoed in the background.

That was the end of the program, so Bradley turned the TV off and relaxed on the sofa. "That Tyler Jensen is one handsome man," he murmured softly. "His character's a real jerk, but I like looking at him anyway."

Matt had finished in the kitchen and had turned on the dishwasher so he wandered into the living room. "What were you watching? I could hear part of it all the way in the kitchen."

"Oh, it was just some situation comedy. It was a rerun from last year, or maybe the year before—*Lucky in Love*. It's kind of cute, I guess."

"You just like the *cute* actor. Pick up your feet, Bradley, so I can sit down with you."

Bradley grinned. "Sure. Would you mind massaging my feet while you're sitting there? You're *so good at it*." He placed his legs and feet across Matt's lap after Matt sat down.

Matt frowned. "Are you sure I wouldn't disturb you?" he asked sarcastically. "I know how tired you must be from all that chewing and lifting your glass during dinner. Not to mention how exhausting it is to watch television."

"Oh, I'll be just fine," Bradley chirped back. "Don't worry about me...."

"All right, Bradley. Enough of this nonsense. We need to talk about tomorrow night."

"Hmmm. How about we cook one of those Italian entrees that we have in the freezer, and then we could watch a movie on TV," Bradley suggested helpfully.

"*Really*? A frozen dinner and TV on New Year's Eve? *Really*?"

"You mean it's New Year's *already*? I thought it was still two or three more days until—"

Matt pulled the pillow out from behind his back and hit Bradley with it. "You better be kidding. You're leaving for California next week and this is our last chance to go out together for a long time and..." Matt sputtered.

Bradley erupted with laughter. "You take everything so *seriously*, sweetheart. Open the drawer of the end table next to you and see what's there!"

Matt did as Bradley instructed. He pouted. "It's just an envelope."

"Perhaps you might look inside."

Matt opened it. "What's this?" he asked.

"It's a brochure, of course. Look it over, and tell me what you think."

"Hampton Luxury Liner? What's that?"

"Honestly, Matt, do I have to do *everything*? It's a bus tour to Atlantic City. I thought a little getaway to a casino for New Year's would be fun."

"I guess it would. Who are you taking?"

"Clarice. She wasn't busy so we're going to celebrate the New Year."

"Ha ha. That's very funny. Then I guess it's a good thing I have a date with Elliot."

Bradley smirked. "I might be worried if he weren't straight."

"All kidding aside, don't you need a reservation for something like this? And I mean quite a bit in advance considering the holiday," Matt said.

"I made the reservations way before this stuff happened at the office. I was going to surprise you with it on Christmas morning until I bought those two gold disks. So I saved this little present until now. I hope you don't mind."

Matt scooted over and gave Bradley a quick kiss. "Of course I don't mind."

"I hope you don't mind the rest of the surprise."

"There's more?"

"I was only halfway kidding about Clarice. She *is* coming too."

Matt looked puzzled. "She's coming *with us* on our trip?"

"Not exactly. When I told her last October about our trip, she decided to get a friend from work to go with her. We'll probably see her on the bus, or maybe once in a while in the casinos, but she won't really be *with us*."

"I love Clarice, of course, but I'm glad she'll have a friend with her. Now we can be together, just the two of us."

"What do you mean?" Bradley asked. "I don't know you, and I won't until we meet on the bus."

Matt laughed.

"I figure we should get on the bus and meet during the bus ride. It would be too hard to meet in a casino since we don't know our way around. Besides, we might hold hands or something on the way," Bradley exclaimed.

"Don't be so hasty," Matt objected. "I might not like you well enough for that. At least not right away."

"Okay," Bradley agreed. "Maybe I'll find some other cute guy on the bus who wants to hold hands...."

"Never mind," Matt scoffed as he pulled his gold disk from inside his shirt. "Just remember what it says on the back."

Bradley grinned again. "Just teasing you, sweetie. I'll always remember."

"TELL me again why we had to leave the apartment at eight forty-five," Matt complained as their cab traveled through the Manhattan morning traffic. "That's kind of early, isn't it?"

Bradley merely gazed at his husband for a moment. "We had to get a cab and get to 45th and Broadway by nine thirty, didn't we? Since the pickup point is right in front of a Starbucks, I thought we should plan for plenty of time to get a cup of coffee before we boarded the bus. Besides, Clarice and her friend are meeting there too."

"What time does the bus leave?"

Bradley pulled the tickets out of his pocket and looked again to be sure. "It says on here we leave at 10:25."

"I guess you're right that we should get there—or should I say *here*, early," Matt replied as the cab arrived at their destination. "I'll pay the cabbie, and you get our bag."

"It's a good thing we're only staying one night," Bradley grumbled as he got out of the cab and looked around for their suitcase, "or we'd have two or three bags instead of just one big one."

Once they were seated inside the Starbucks with their coffee, Bradley and Matt saw Clarice and a chunky red-haired young man waving and coming toward their table, coffee cups in hand.

"Hi, *Bratt*," Clarice called out with a huge smile on her face. "This is Charlie. We work together at the library."

Bradley turned to Matt and whispered, "When you said a friend from work, I thought you meant a girl."

"So did I," Matt whispered back. "Shhh. Here they are."

After explaining the Bratt nickname, Clarice introduced Bradley and Matt to Charlie. Then Clarice and Charlie sat down with them.

"I've never been to Atlantic City," Charlie said. "I've really been looking forward to this."

"We've never been before either," Matt replied. "I didn't even know about this trip until yesterday. Bradley bought the tickets as an extra Christmas present."

"I can't believe you kept it a secret for so long," Clarice said to Bradley. "I wanted to tell him, but I didn't give in to temptation."

"Are we all going to try to sit together on the bus?" Charlie asked. "No offense, but I sort of hoped to be alone with Clarice."

Matt and Bradley chuckled.

"No. Don't worry. And Bradley and I are going to meet each other for the first time on the bus," Matt said. At Charlie's puzzled look, he explained about the cheating game.

Charlie gave Clarice a quizzical look, but Clarice just laughed. "It's an idea I gave them from something I saw on TV. I'll tell you all about it on the way."

"How do you want to do this?" Matt asked Bradley.

"I've been giving it some thought. How about you get on the bus first, I'll wait about two or three minutes, and then I'll find where you're sitting. I'll join you, and we'll introduce ourselves."

"Okay," Matt agreed. "Sounds like a plan. And it's a good thing we've decided because it looks like the bus is here."

They all scrambled to get their bags and made their way toward the bus, where a line had already formed. Clarice and Charlie went first and boarded together. Next Matt got on the bus and found two unoccupied seats about halfway down the aisle, several rows from Clarice and Charlie. At last, after handing the driver their bag to be loaded underneath the bus, Bradley climbed the steps and started toward where Matt was sitting.

Suddenly, a middle-aged portly man stopped by Matt's seat. "Is this seat taken?"

Before Matt could answer, the man sat down and started to unbutton his coat.

"Just a minute, sir," Matt protested. "I was saving that seat for someone."

"Too late," the man replied. "You should have said something before I sat down."

"You didn't give me a chance."

Bradley arrived, looking very annoyed. He looked at Matt in exasperation.

Matt turned to the man and smiled. "Well, I guess it's all right for you to sit there."

Now Bradley flushed and glared at them both, but Matt and the man just ignored him.

"You've got to keep this a secret if I tell you," Matt whispered to the man.

"Keep *what* a secret? What are you talking about?"

Matt smiled innocently. "Well, I've brought my medication so maybe it'll be all right. The doctor said I was still contagious, but I'm wearing this heavy coat that covers me up."

The man looked alarmed now. "What do you mean? Do you have a disease or something?"

"It's just that today is New Year's Eve, and I had already bought my ticket. I just couldn't sit home all alone tonight, could I?"

With fear in his eyes, the man asked, "What do you have? Tell me."

Matt grinned mischievously. "It's only shingles. You probably won't get it." He began rubbing his hands together. "I don't think there are many germs left."

As quickly as he could, the man jumped up and fled down the aisle to another seat as far from Matt as he could get.

"Is this seat taken, sir?" Bradley asked, looking more than a little relieved.

"No. Go ahead and sit down," Matt replied as though he didn't know Bradley.

"Thanks," Bradley replied and sat down. He turned to Matt and asked in a low voice, "What was all that whispering about?"

"I beg your pardon? That's none of your business."

"All right, Matt. Cough it up. What was going on with that guy who had my seat?"

"Play the game, Bradley. I'll tell you all about it later," Matt whispered back.

Bradley cleared his throat and sat quietly for a moment. Then he turned toward Matt. "Uh… hello. Since we'll be traveling for about three hours together, I thought I should introduce myself. I'm a businessman here in New York, on my way to spend the holiday at Resorts Casino. My name is Mustard. Colonel Mustard, to be exact."

Matt laughed. "Really? Did you leave the candlestick or the lead pipe in the library?"

The colonel merely smiled. "Cute. That's very cute. People tease me about my name all the time."

"I hope they don't *die* laughing," Matt replied with a grin. "Your name is quite a coincidence, actually."

"Oh? How do you mean?"

"Well, curiously enough I share a famous name too. I'm a college professor in New York. My name is Plum. Professor Plum."

"Oh, very nicely done," Colonel Mustard replied with a chuckle. "I can tell that we're going to get along famously."

"That's the word, all right," Professor Plum agreed, patting the colonel on the cheek.

"I hope you don't think that I'm being too familiar, *stranger that you are*, I mean," Colonel Mustard began, scooting closer to the professor. "But I think you're a very attractive man. For a plum, uh... *Professor Plum*, that is."

The professor smiled at the colonel. "I was examining you too," he replied. "You're the most attractive Mustard I've ever met." He took the colonel's hand and kissed it. "Spicy too."

"How about a drink?" the colonel suggested. "Did you notice the bar in the back of the bus?"

The professor smiled. "I did, but it's a little early for me to have a cocktail. Perhaps some coffee would be nice."

THAT night after an evening at the gaming tables in the casino, Matt and Bradley lay naked in each other's arms in their queen-size hotel bed.

Matt glanced at the clock. "It's close to midnight. We'd better get downstairs to the main bar to meet Clarice and Charlie. They'll be disappointed if we don't all greet the new year together."

Bradley looked dubious. "I'm not so sure about that, sweetheart. Charlie wouldn't mind if we didn't show up at all. I think he really likes Clarice."

"Maybe so. But then *I'll* be the one disappointed not to share the moment with Clarice at least."

"You mean I'm not enough for you?" Bradley asked with a grin.

"Oh, don't be silly. You know what I mean. We've got the rest of the night to be together, but I'd like to be there for the countdown. And I love to hear everybody drunkenly singing 'Auld Lang Syne' at midnight."

"Well, let's hurry and get dressed, then," Bradley agreed.

"Did you notice how strangely Charlie has treated us since we got here?" Matt asked as he pulled on his shirt and pants.

Bradley laughed. "Didn't Clarice tell you? That guy who tried to sit with you told everyone on the bus that you were contagious with the shingles."

Matt stared at Bradley who was trying to tie his necktie. "*Really*? Wow. Maybe I went too far, but I had to get rid of him."

"Clarice tried to explain it all to Charlie, but I think he's still a little afraid to get very close to you. I wouldn't give him a New Year's kiss if I were you."

Now Matt laughed. "I hadn't planned to do that. Not to change the subject, but what casino game did you like best?"

"I guess I liked shooting craps a lot, but blackjack was fun too."

Matt put on his shoes. "I think I liked roulette the best. It was kind of hard to catch on to the many ways to place a bet, but I enjoyed it when I learned how to play."

Bradley raised his eyebrows. "I thought you would say you liked the dollar slots the best since you won five hundred dollars."

Matt laughed again. "Well, that was fun all right, but it was just a fluke. I had a few extra dollar bills in my wallet, and that machine sort of *called to me*."

"Oh yeah? I didn't hear one call out to me. Are you ready to go?"

"Just about, I guess. Bradley, come here a second. I want to give you a private New Year's kiss before we go downstairs." He paused and looked in Bradley's eyes. "I love you so much, Bradley."

"And you already know how much I love you back. So I'll take that kiss *right now*."

Chapter
TWELVE

MATT knocked on Kristen's office door next to his and waited for a response.

"Is that you, Matt?" a voice called. "Come on in… it's not locked."

"Good morning," Matt greeted her as he entered. "Ready for class?"

She looked up from her desk and smiled. "Sure. I'll just grab my briefcase and walk with you down the hall."

"What class do you have first this morning?" she asked as she closed the office door and glanced at her watch.

"I've got twentieth century British history and then the second half of Western civilization right after lunch. What about you?"

Kristen laughed. "I've got your favorite—History of Africa."

Matt shook his head. "I always dread my turn at teaching that class because it's so hard to work everything in. There's so much content that covers so many civilizations over a lot of centuries. It's hard to do the subject justice in a semester course. They ought to divide it up into two courses."

"I'm with you," she agreed. "The last time I had to teach this class, I only just barely made it into the twentieth century." She paused and then said, "Not to change the subject, but how is Bradley doing?"

"Fine, I think. I talked to him last night on the phone, and he said things are okay so far. He and his friend Elliot are sharing an efficiency place for the time being. It's one of those extended stay hotels that you rent by the month."

"He's staying with another guy? Are you all right with that?"

Matt laughed. "You haven't met Elliot, I guess. He's the straight guy who was Bradley's roommate in college. As a matter of fact, he was best man at our wedding so he's harmless. With Bradley, anyway," he added with a grin.

"I see. It sounds like a smart idea since Bradley won't be there but for a few months."

"Exactly," Matt agreed. "It will also give Elliot a chance to find a more permanent apartment or house without having to rush into it."

Kristen turned to look more directly into Matt's eyes. "The real question is how are *you* doing?"

"Me? I'm fine, I suppose."

"You know what I mean. How are you getting along with Bradley being in California?"

This time Matt frowned. "I'm okay, all things considered. It gets lonely in the apartment at night. Well, really it gets lonely all the time."

"You should get out some. Try keeping busy while he's gone."

"If you mean like going out to bars or something like that...."

"No," Kristen objected. "I didn't mean that. Go out to dinner, or to the movies, or shopping. You've got lots of friends to help you stay occupied."

"You're right. So when are you and I going for dinner and a movie?"

Kristen paused and then slowly shook her head. "Well, I can't this weekend. But how about next week?"

"That sounds pretty good to me," Matt agreed. "We'll talk later and firm up our plans."

They reached Kristen's classroom door. "I've got a luncheon date today so maybe we can figure out a plan later this afternoon," she replied. "See you later—"

"Okay. Bye." Matt turned to walk to his classroom across the hall and did not notice the man who had followed the two professors all the way down the hall. The unseen man quickly turned around and went back the other way, smiling as he walked.

"WAKE up, sleepyhead."

Bradley groaned and tried to read the red digital numbers on the clock on the nightstand. Finally he blinked rapidly and focused on 7:01

a.m. through partially closed eyelids. He sat up, looking around the room for Elliot.

"It's only seven," Bradley complained in the general direction of the voice he'd heard.

"Don't you remember that we have to meet Winston at eight?" Elliot reminded him. "He's got a temporary office rented, but we have to meet him there and then go look at larger available office space for the new firm."

"I wonder why he only asked the two of us to help him. The other partners aren't even coming out here to LA for a couple of weeks."

"We just got lucky, I guess," Elliot said with a smirk. "Seriously, he said he particularly wanted *my input* since I've been here before. Ha. That's pretty funny. I was only here for your and Matt's wedding."

"Yeah, that really gave you some California experience all right," Bradley laughed.

"Evidently he's forgotten that you were here at the same time. He won't admit it, but I bet he thinks of you as Grace's spy. He knows she has final approval of what he does out here."

"I suppose you're right. It certainly wouldn't do her any good to come traipsing out here to LA before she's fully recovered." Bradley watched Elliot pour himself a cup of coffee in the miniature kitchen of their tiny apartment, and he jumped out of bed and sped to the bathroom. "First dibs on the shower," he sang out as he slammed the door.

MATT ended his class early after assigning some chapters to be read for next time, and then he glanced through the window of Kristen's classroom door. She was absorbed in her lecture. He sighed and ambled back down the hall to his office.

"Darn," he muttered as he noticed he'd left the lights on. "Double darn," he added as the doorknob turned easily. "I forgot to lock the office, and I bet Kristen did the same thing." He was right. Her office door opened too. He closed it and returned to his own office to drop off his briefcase.

"I guess I'll go over to the student union and have lunch in the faculty cafeteria. Hmmm. I wonder if talking to myself is part of missing Bradley. And I better not start answering myself, or this will get serious." He laughed softly.

Then he noticed a folded sheet of paper with a heart drawn on it. Inside the heart was his first name. It had been placed under the box of pens and pencils on his desk, and he knew that it had not been there earlier this morning. Curiously, he pulled the paper out and unfolded it. There was a note, printed in black block letters. *YOU DON'T HAVE TO BE LONELY!*

The words stunned Matt. Who except for a few of his faculty friends knew he was alone while his husband had gone west? Students who sometimes played pranks usually showed a little humor, but this wasn't funny. It wasn't even cute.

"Well, I could stand here and puzzle over this piece of paper, but I still wouldn't solve the mystery. I guess I'll go to lunch. Oops. I'm talking out loud again," he mused.

This time he turned out the lights and carefully locked the door before leaving his office.

"I WASN'T terribly impressed with anything the agent showed us today," Winston grumbled to Elliot and Bradley. "What did you two think?" he asked as he closed the door to their temporary office and sat down at the only desk in the room.

Bradley stretched out as best he could in an office chair that was only moderately comfortable. "I agree with you, Winston, but we can't take too long to select a location. With the rest of the staff arriving in a couple of weeks, we're going to be 'under construction', so to speak, even when they get here so a delay in finding office space just makes it worse."

"He's right, Winston," Elliot agreed. "You'd better make that agent get serious about finding us a place. I think he's just trying to pawn off his worst properties, hoping to make a bigger profit."

Winston nodded. "You're both exactly right, and I'm going to go straight to the head of the agency to make it clear that we'll go elsewhere, and *fast*, if they can't help us."

Elliot sat down in the chair next to Bradley while Winston chewed out the agency's owner on the phone. "Want to go out to eat at a nice restaurant tonight?"

"Sure. Funny you should mention it, but I was looking online for really good restaurants just last night. I found one that looks interesting. It's in the Hollywood Hills so it's not too far from our place. It's called Yamashiro, or something like that. The video ad I saw said it was Asian-inspired and California-creative."

"You're really getting into this casual West Coast stuff, aren't you?"

"Well, it sounded interesting to me. And I have to tell you, Elliot, it still surprises me how much I like these California restaurants. I guess I'm a New York snob, but I didn't think I'd like it out here at all. Anyway, take a look at the ad on your phone and see what you think."

After several tries to get the spelling right, Elliot did just that. "It looks pretty good, but could we get a reservation on such short notice?"

"Beats me. We can only try. Since it's a weeknight, maybe we can get in. Winston's off the phone. Ask him if he wants to go too."

"Hey, Winston. Want to go out tonight to a really decent place? And I don't mean Denny's."

Winston smiled. "I think I got their attention at last. Tomorrow we're finally going to see some better possibilities. Dinner? Sure. It'll give me something nice to tell Harriet when I call her later. As it is, she's not really all that crazy about leaving New York."

"I'll call for reservations," Bradley volunteered. "I bet Matt will be interested to hear about something more exciting than just potential offices."

HIS second and final class for the day finished, Matt gathered up his notes and books to put into his briefcase. He glanced at the departing students, but there was nothing unusual to catch his eye, and none of them appeared to even look his way. It grew quiet now with the classroom empty except for him. At last Matt picked up the briefcase and made his way out to the hall where he paused for a moment, looking to see if anyone waited for him.

Suspicious because of the mysterious note, Matt walked cautiously toward his office. With an effort to appear casual and unconcerned, he turned his gaze from student to student as he walked. Nothing seemed out of the ordinary. One student, leaning up against a wall and apparently waiting for his next class, turned to look at Matt. But it was only for a moment, and his gaze quickly shifted away. Two others, both girls who looked vaguely familiar, smiled at him while they spoke to each other as he went by. Probably they were former students, he thought.

"I'm getting paranoid about that note," he muttered. "And I've got to stop talking to myself," he added quietly as he neared his office. Before he could stop himself, he said softly, "For heaven's sake, it was probably just a note from a fellow professor. But that's absurd. No professor would write something like that. And even if a *student* did leave it, there was nothing malicious about it."

Matt unlocked his office and turned on the lights once more. Nothing looked out of order, but then the office had been locked this time. He decided to revise his notes for a class the next day. A bell had rung a few minutes before, which signaled that another class period had begun. The halls were quiet now so Matt was able to concentrate and adjust his notes.

Absorbed in his work, he barely noticed the passage of time and became more and more relaxed in the soothing silence of his office. Convinced finally that he was more than prepared for tomorrow's class, he put his papers away and leaned back in his chair. He closed his eyes and felt peaceful for the first time since early this morning.

The jarring ring of the telephone on his desk startled him. He took a calming breath and answered. "Doctor Sharp," he said in his businesslike voice.

"You don't have to be alone," a male voice replied soothingly.

Matt almost dropped the phone. "*Who is this?*" he managed to gasp. "What do you want?"

"I'm someone who finds you attractive and utterly desirable," the voice said. "And I only want to comfort you and keep you company. We could have a really good time together—"

"I don't know you, and I don't want to know you. Wait a minute. Is this Gerald? If that's who you are, you need to stop calling and leaving me notes in my office—I'm *not* going to change that grade."

"Calm down, handsome. Let's forget about grades. You don't realize how good I could make you feel with you in my arms and with my tongue in your mouth and my hands all over your hard—"

Almost strangled from fear, Matt gulped and slammed the receiver down, not knowing how pale he looked. He decided to call security so he looked up the number and dialed. After being put on hold, he finally got an officer who was available to take his call.

"This is Officer Donnally. How can I help you?"

"I'm Dr. Matthew Sharp in the history department. I'd like to report a case of possible harassment."

"Could you give me the details please, Dr. Sharp?"

Matt went through the entire story of the mysterious note left in his office and the anonymous caller. He was distressed but not surprised to learn that the call could not be traced at this point, and while security would analyze the note, it was doubtful it would help unless they found fingerprints. Even that would be a long shot. Fingerprints might be difficult to identify, despite involving the New York police.

"Since there was no obvious threat, Dr. Sharp, and from what you've said—there's only the note as hard evidence to go on—I don't think there is much that we can do, other than check on this student named Gerald Winthrop. At the moment, anyway. You might be right that he's the one playing a prank on you. We'll try to find out, and we'll send someone to your office for the note to see what we can discover. In the meantime, please keep us informed if there are any further developments."

"Thank you, Officer Donnally. I'll do that. Are you sending someone over this afternoon?"

"Yes. I'll take care of it immediately. Between you and me, Dr. Sharp, I wouldn't worry about this too much. This is a college campus, and students can sometimes do silly and meaningless things. Try to relax and put it out of your mind unless something else more serious happens. If your former student is indeed involved, I'm sure we can put enough fear in him to stop his antics."

"Thank you again, Officer Donnally. Goodbye."

Well, that was probably a waste of time. But at least I can call Bradley and tell him all about it. That would make me feel much better. Bradley will know what to do.

He pulled out his cell phone and called Bradley's number. The phone rang once and went to voice mail. "Leave a message," Bradley's voice cheerfully requested.

"Bradley, it's me. Please call me back as soon as you get this message. Something really odd is going on, and I'm more than a little worried. Thanks."

"I hope he doesn't wait too long to return my call," Matt said out loud as he ended the call. "I've got to stop talking out loud, or it'll become a habit. Then people really *will* think I'm crazy."

HOURS later Matt sat on the sofa in Clarice's apartment, having just told her the story of the note, the phone call, the two encounters with Gerald Winthrop, and his own call to campus security. "It's just too weird, Clarice."

"It certainly is," Clarice said. "But I'm not sure if it's serious or just a joke of some kind."

"Well, it's not a very funny joke, if that's what it is," Matt complained. "That phone call really scared me. And if that kid is trying to get even with me over his low grade, he's doing a very good job of it."

"I'm trying to be careful here," she hedged. "If there's nothing to it, I don't want to make you all upset over the whole thing. On the other hand, if it's a serial killer lurking around waiting to slit your throat, I'd hate to be the one who told you to ignore it."

"Oh, *thanks*, Clarice. I feel so much better," Matt replied sarcastically.

Clarice hugged Matt, who was sitting next to her. "I'm sorry. I didn't mean to scare you. But in a way, it's kind of like we're in a *Scream* movie or something."

Matt pulled back and glared at her. "You're not helping, Clarice."

"Look at it this way, Matt honey. The note and call happened in your office so it must have something to do with school. And that student talked to you at school—not away from the campus. You didn't have anything strange happen at home, did you?"

"No," Matt admitted. "I see your point. And I've already called security on campus, as I told you, so I'll be talking to them if anything else happens."

"Good thinking. And you're never really all that much alone there anyway. There are students and other professors all around you. You'll be okay." She patted him on the shoulder.

"I take it back. You *are* making me feel a little better." He smiled a little cautiously. "But I still think I'll tell Bradley about it when he finally calls me, though."

"WOW. You've either got a stalker, a vengeful former student, or a fanatic admirer," Bradley exclaimed.

"You say that last one like it's a conquest or something to be proud of," Matt objected. "I told you how much it scared me when I got that phone call in my office. The note wasn't nearly as frightening. Now that I think about the former student, I'm having a hard time imagining him saying the things that the caller did."

Bradley recognized the anxiety in Matt's voice. "I'm sorry, sweetheart. I shouldn't be making fun. Do you want me to fly back to New York this weekend and stay with you?"

"Of course I'd enjoy seeing you," Matt replied, "but not just to babysit with me because of what happened. Clarice calmed me down a lot when she pointed out that there really wasn't a threat—at least not exactly. And it must somehow be related to school. Even campus security thinks it was probably just some student's idea of a joke."

"I'm not trying to make light of the whole thing, but I think Clarice is right. I doubt if you really have anything to worry about, but I'll come home if you want me to."

"No, Bradley. You've only been gone for a couple of weeks and you were planning to come back for Valentine's Day anyway. And that's only three or four weeks away. I'll be all right."

"That's true, and you'll be flying out here a few weeks after that during your spring break. We'll make up for lost time then."

"Maybe I've just been overreacting to the whole thing. I bet nothing else happens, and we can laugh about it when we finally do get together."

"Just remember to keep your office locked when you're not there... and maybe when you *are* there by yourself," Bradley warned. "If that Gerald guy comes anywhere near you, I think I'd report him."

"Oh, I will. And you can bet I'll keep the office locked up tight too. I'm sure the unlocked door is how the guy got into my office to leave that note. It would have been easy for the caller to get the office extension—from the campus directory or even the school's website. It's not that hard to contact a faculty member at school."

"It would be another thing if you were getting calls on your cell phone or at the apartment...."

"That's for sure," Matt agreed. "If that were to happen, I'd have to get a lot more serious and ask the *real* police for help. But that's not likely. Now tell me all about the fun you're having in California. Have you met any sexy movie stars yet?"

Bradley laughed. "Not many. Just five or six. I've had dates almost every night."

"Well, I guess I'd better get busy and do the same thing here in New York. I can't let you get ahead of me. Maybe I could hang around the stage entrances on Broadway."

This time Bradley just chuckled a little. "Back to reality, Matt. I've been really busy with this business of finding an office. Winston doesn't exactly let Elliot and me go to Disneyland or Knott's Berry Farm every day. We've been to a couple of nice restaurants, but that's about it for social life. But I hope to find some fun places to take you when you're here during spring break. Just remember that any investigating along those lines is just for *your* benefit, sweetheart."

"I'm very sure we'll... ah... find *something* to do when we get together," Matt said.

"You're so right, sweetie," Bradley agreed lustily. "But I'll show you the town anyway."

"I can't wait."

"Me neither, but I guess I'd better go for now. I don't want to keep you on the phone too late on a school night."

Matt giggled. "That's right, *Mother*. I'm getting off the phone right now."

"I love you."

"Love you back."

Chapter
THIRTEEN

ELLIOT knocked on the door, and then without waiting for a reply, he walked into Bradley's new temporary office in the suite of offices that Winston had chosen at last.

"I guess those decorators realized that Winston meant business when he said to get this place ready for us, effective last week. This is a snazzy office, Bradley. Maybe you should think about keeping it and staying out here in LA."

Bradley looked up from the papers on his desk and smiled ruefully. "I don't even have to tell you the two reasons why I can't do that—Matt and Grace."

Elliot grinned at his friend. "But admit it, Bradley. You know you *like* it out here. And I think Winston is becoming as attached to you as Grace is. I bet he'd like for you to stay."

"I do admit that I like California a lot more than I thought I would. The weather is so much better in LA than in New York during the winter, and I've enjoyed the restaurants out here, too. But that still doesn't change anything. There's Matt to consider. You know that as well as I do."

Elliot sat down in front of Bradley's desk and stretched out. "I know. And I get it. Still, if you could somehow—"

"Stop right there. Let's change the subject. What do you want to do tonight, roomie?"

"How about our usual routine—dinner at some nice restaurant? We could even look for one in West Hollywood. You know, so you'd feel at home with the *other* gay boys."

"If we weren't friends, Elliot, I'd take that as an insult and an outrageous put-down. And I might even punch you out," he added with a grin.

Elliot laughed. "But since we *are* such good friends, you know I was only slightly teasing you about being lonely without Matt."

"I realize that and appreciate the sentiment. However, I have a feeling that Matt would like it better if you and I went out with some pretty young aspiring actresses and left the good-looking Hollywood guys alone."

"Now that's an idea I'd fully support," Elliot replied with a grin. "But since we don't know anyone except the ladies from the firm, let's at least go to a good restaurant. You can sit at the table after dinner and have a drink while looking like your usual sexy self, and I'll go see if there are some interesting ladies at the bar."

"Okay, I guess. Just today I was looking online for a new place to eat and found one called—"

"Wait a minute, trendy tourist. Is this one of those places where you have to make a reservation a year ahead, know somebody with clout, or somehow sneak onto the 'list' to get in? That's not my favorite kind of restaurant,"

Bradley laughed. "There's a Burger King close to our place."

"You don't have to go to the other extreme. Let's just find a nice place to eat and let it go at that."

A knock sounded at the door.

"Come in," Bradley called and was not at all surprised to see Winston stroll in and sit down next to Elliot.

His face wore a frown at the moment. He glanced at Elliot first, and then he fixed his gaze on Bradley behind his desk.

"I hope you two can help me out with a small dilemma. This evening I had planned to meet with one of our new clients over dinner. I had reservations and was about to leave for home to get ready when my wife called and reminded me that we're having a small dinner party at our place for some *other* clients. I can't believe I forgot all about it, but I did."

"So you want one of us to meet the new client for dinner?" Elliot asked.

"Well, yes," Winston replied. "One or both of you, if that's possible. It's just a courtesy dinner to put the client at ease, welcome him aboard, and give him a feel for our services. Nothing too demanding or detailed is expected."

"Who is this new client?" Bradley asked.

"Perhaps he's someone familiar to you," Winston replied. "He's a popular TV actor, I hear. I'm not exactly up on all the recent programs so I don't really know who he is. He's in some sort of contract dispute or other and wants our counsel."

"Who is it?" Elliot asked.

"His name is Tyler Jensen. Maybe you've seen his show. I've forgotten the name of it."

Bradley grinned broadly. "I know who he is. He's in a situation comedy called *Lucky in Love*. I've seen it a few times. It's kind of funny... once in a while."

"Is it that silly show where the guy dates a bunch of different girls who don't know about each other?" Elliot asked.

"That's the one," Bradley confirmed.

"I tried to watch that one time, and it was so dumb I switched the channel."

"You don't have to tell *him* that, Elliot," Bradley admonished. "Just smile a lot and tell him his show is a lot of fun."

"That's the spirit," Winston agreed, the frown slipping from his face. "So you'll both help me out, then?"

"Sure," Bradley assured him. "We'd love to, wouldn't we, Elliot?"

"Of course. We were just discussing dinner plans when you came in. You've solved our problem, boss."

Winston smiled and rose. "Thank you, gentlemen. I do appreciate this. Now I need to get home and get myself ready for my own dinner guests. Have a nice evening."

"Where are we going?" Bradley asked. "You didn't say."

"Oh, of course. It's called Haute. You'll find the address on this," Winston added, handing Bradley a business card. "I wrote the address and phone number on the back of one of my business cards. And the reservations are in the name of the firm so there's no problem there. Once again, have a good time." He left the office.

"Hmmm. Looks like we get to meet our first Hollywood star," Bradley announced with a smile. "And since he has quite a reputation with the ladies, I'm sure he'll help you meet an attractive starlet or two."

Elliot brightened at the thought. "Maybe you're right. Let's get out of here and prepare ourselves for what might be our best evening in LA yet."

"JUST this way, gentlemen," the maître d' announced as he led Elliot and Bradley toward what looked like one of the best tables at Haute. "Mr. Jensen only just arrived a few minutes ago."

"Thanks," Elliot responded. He turned around and asked Bradley under his breath, "Do I tip the guy for this?"

"It's a high-class joint," Bradley laughed softly. "Give him a twenty, just to be on the safe side. We might have to come back here again sometime. I'm even thinking that Matt would like to see this place when he's here for a visit in a few weeks. Look at that *view* through those windows."

Elliot nodded and palmed a bill to the maître d' as they reached the table. A strikingly good-looking man sat waiting and sipping a cocktail. He smiled when he saw Bradley and Elliot and quickly rose to offer his hand in greeting.

"Good evening, gentlemen," he said with a broad smile. "I'm Tyler Jensen."

Bradley grinned and then introduced himself and Elliot. "Of course, I'd recognize you from your TV show. I've enjoyed it many times."

"You're very kind," Tyler replied, still smiling. "Do sit down and join me. Winston, if I may be so familiar about someone I've only met briefly, tells me that you two are his best and favorite associates, so I've been looking forward to meeting you."

"That's nice to hear," Elliot said, sitting on one side of Tyler while Bradley sat down on the other. "Of course, Winston will probably want to go into greater detail about your contract when he meets with you in the office tomorrow."

"Naturally," Tyler agreed. "We won't really get into all of that this evening."

At that moment a waiter arrived. "Good evening, gentlemen, and welcome to Haute. My name is Jeffrey, and I'll be your server this evening. Have you had a chance to look over the menu?"

"We just got here," Bradley replied. "Give us a few more minutes."

"Certainly, sir. I'll check back with you shortly," Jeffrey said. "In the meantime, may I get any of you something from the bar?"

Tyler glanced at Bradley and Elliot who both shook their heads. "Not just yet... we'll let you know."

A little later, orders placed and colorful tropical drinks on the table, Bradley and Elliot relaxed and began to unwind from the workday.

"So, are you originally from LA?" Bradley asked.

Tyler laughed. "I don't know anyone who's really from LA. I'm from Seattle, and everyone else seems to be from all sorts of places. Even New York," he added with a grin.

"It's kind of like that in New York, in a way. But there really *are* a lot of real New Yorkers around. That includes me." Bradley smiled.

Elliot leaned over to Tyler and asked softly, "Where's the men's room? I need to make a little trip."

Tyler smiled and pointed over Elliot's shoulder. "Right through there. You can't miss it."

"Thanks," Elliot murmured. "I won't be long."

Tyler turned to Bradley, and his eyes looked searchingly into Bradley's for perhaps a moment too long. "Are you enjoying your stay so far?"

Feeling slightly uncomfortable from the intense gaze, Bradley said, "Sure. I guess so, anyway. We haven't had much time to do anything but get our new offices organized."

"No time for... uh... *personal pleasures*?"

"Not really. We've been awfully busy."

"In that case," Tyler said, taking out a little leather case from his coat pocket and removing a business card, "let me give you this." He wrote something on the back and handed it to Bradley. "This is my personal cell phone number. Call me sometime, and I'd be happy to show you around to... say... some of the more *interesting places* not always seen by ordinary tourists or visitors."

Bradley looked a little puzzled as he studied Tyler's grinning face. "Are you trying to tell me something, Tyler? It's more of a rhetorical question actually."

Tyler grinned. "My, uh, gaydar told me we might have something uh, in common."

Now Bradley studied Tyler more closely for a few minutes. "What if you're wrong? Our professional relationship would be compromised."

"Am I wrong?" Tyler asked. "I'm usually pretty good at judging... *character*."

"No. You guessed correctly, but—"

"So don't worry about it, Bradley. You're not going to be the one handling my account anyway. Winston made it very clear that he would take care of any business. It was my understanding that you and Elliot were merely introducing me to the firm in his absence at another function. I just thought you and I could be... special... social friends. That's all."

"Even so, you take me by surprise," Bradley said. He put his elbows on the table as he brought his hands up near his face, seemingly to rest his chin against them. However, he made sure to put his left hand over his right.

Tyler grinned even more broadly. "I see that you want to make sure your wedding band is quite prominent," he said softly. "Is it for real, or is it part of a disguise at the office?"

This time Bradley smiled back. "It's for real. Here... let me show you." He took out his wallet and flashed a photo of his handsome husband. "His name is Matt, and we actually got married here in LA a few years ago."

"You certainly made an excellent choice," Tyler replied, looking up from the photo with a grin. "He's really quite cute. My compliments."

"Thanks, and yes, he is," Bradley replied, putting his wallet away. "And there's no disguise. Everyone at the office knows about us. Elliot was even our best man at the wedding."

Tyler chuckled. "I envy you. Here in Hollywood it's not so easy to be out and open about it. The public doesn't always appreciate such personal honesty."

"Well, I'm just fortunate to have very understanding bosses," Bradley replied.

Tyler gazed at Bradley with what appeared to be new respect. "Hey, just because I tried to pick you up doesn't mean we can't be friends. The offer still stands."

Bradley frowned and started to shake his head. "I don't know...."

"No. Seriously. I promise to behave. It's just that you're a really good-looking guy. I thought it wouldn't hurt to give it a shot with you, even though I did see the ring right away."

"I guess it would be fun to go out for a drink sometime. Matt wouldn't mind, I'm sure. But I'll tell you this. Elliot is going to be really disappointed. He believes your image from your TV show and thinks that you can help him meet a few gorgeous girls, especially actresses."

Tyler laughed again. "I try to be as good an actor as I can be, so I'm glad to hear that."

"Oh, I believed it too. I was really more than a little shocked when I saw that you're not really the character you portray on the show. But of course it's just TV."

"Exactly," Tyler agreed. "Here he comes. Shall we tell him the truth? I trust that client-attorney privilege applies among the three of us?"

Bradley hesitated. "It does. But no, let him have his little fantasy about meeting pretty stars... at least for a little while longer."

"Okay. We'll play it your way. But surely you understand that I actually *do* have a number of quite beautiful actress acquaintances. And I'd be glad to introduce Elliot." He smiled again. "Do think about it, and give me a call soon. Then you and I will go out—as friends, of course."

MATT'S cell phone rang in the darkness. He abruptly sat up in bed, frightened out of his deep sleep. He turned to the nightstand, where the tiny light from the phone shattered the early morning gloom.

"What if it's that creep who called before?" he asked himself out loud in breathy tones. "But how could he get my cell number?"

Reluctantly, he reached out for the phone and looked at the number on the screen. He breathed a sigh of relief and pushed the answer button.

"Hi, Bradley. Is something wrong?"

"Not at all. What makes you ask that?" Bradley replied.

"Well, it *is* after one in the morning," Matt reminded him as he glanced at the glowing red numbers on the bedside alarm clock.

"Damn. I keep forgetting the time change. It's only just past ten o'clock here."

"I'm glad to hear from you, despite the time. But what's up that you called so late?"

"I'm afraid I have a little bad news, Matt. I won't be able to fly to New York for Valentine's Day after all. I'm so sorry, sweetheart. But it falls in the middle of the week, and I just can't get away except on a weekend." He paused. "I was really looking forward to it too."

Matt sighed and then attempted to hide his disappointment. "It's okay, Bradley. I understand. Besides, I'll be with you pretty soon out there in LA during our spring break."

"That's the spirit, honey. It won't be long—you'll see."

"But is that what you woke me up to tell me? You could have called tomorrow. Is there something else going on that I should know about?"

Bradley giggled and hesitated for effect. "Well, there *is* one more thing... I just couldn't wait to tell you that I had my first date with a Hollywood star. And I would never have dreamed someone would try to pick me up for... uh, well... you know. A little cozy date for later."

Matt frowned. "What was that again?"

"I said I just had a date with a TV star tonight. We went out for dinner and drinks."

"Well, aren't you the man-about-town. Do I know her?"

"Did I say 'her'?" Bradley asked, apparently drawing out his story as long as he could.

"Oh, you went out with a *guy*? You're being very mysterious about this. Who was it?"

"Somebody you've seen on TV who likes to fool around with lots of different girls."

Matt paused to think about this. Then it hit him. "You had dinner with *Tyler Jensen?*"

"That's the one. I knew you'd get it."

"It must have been odd for you to sit with him while all the girls in the place tried to mob your table. And which one tried to pick you up?"

"Oh, it wasn't like that at all. It was a very quiet evening, and he was quite the gentleman. Besides, Elliot was there too."

"That's nice," Matt said, somewhat relieved. "But who tried to pick you up?" he asked again.

Bradley drew a deep breath, again trying to keep Matt in suspense. "It was *Tyler*. He asked me to go barhopping with him sometime."

"Why would he do that?"

"Don't be so naïve, sweetheart. Surely you can figure that out."

Again Matt thought for a moment. "He's *gay?* That stud act with the ladies on TV isn't for real?"

"I just *knew* you'd be able to solve it," Bradley replied, laughing softly.

This time there was an edge to Matt's voice as he replied coldly, "That's kind of mean to tell me this after the Valentine's Day business."

"I'm sorry about the timing, sweetie—"

"What were you doing with him in the first place? And what did you answer when he asked you out?"

"My goodness. So many questions. I think my trusting husband is getting a little jealous."

"All right, Bradley. Let's have the story. I can tell that you put a lot of thought into figuring out the best way to tease me about this date of yours." He chuckled. "Out with it."

Bradley stopped giggling and replied. "Okay. Here's the story. Tyler is one of Winston's new clients. Winston asked Elliot and me to wine and dine him this evening because he was otherwise occupied. There really wasn't that much to it. While Elliot was in the restroom, Tyler came out to me. But you don't have to worry, sweetheart. I pulled out a photo of you from my wallet, flashed my wedding ring, and politely turned him down. If I hadn't been wearing a tie, I would have pulled out the medallion around my neck to show it to him."

"That was a nice touch, Bradley." Matt made a smooching sound into the phone. "There's a little kiss for you. Of course, I trusted you all along. I just wanted to hear the whole story. And naturally you seemed determined to make it as *dramatic* as possible. That was obvious."

"You have to agree that it makes a good story. But remember that attorney-client privilege is in effect with Tyler so you can't go tell Clarice or anyone else that he's gay! I could get into trouble for even letting *you* know."

"Now, Bradley, you know that I don't spill office secrets. My lips are sealed."

"They better stay that way until I get the chance to open them up with a big kiss. And then with something else."

It was Matt's turn to giggle. "I can't wait. It's only a couple of weeks, you know."

"I'm counting the days until you get off the plane at LAX."

"Oh, you sound so *California* the way you say that."

"This place is getting into my blood more than I thought it would. By the way, have you had any more of those mysterious phone calls or visits from that creepy ex-student?"

"No. There's nothing new about any of that. The campus cops checked on Gerald Winthrop, and he had an airtight alibi for when that call came."

"Maybe that's all there was to it, and you won't be bothered again."

"I hope you're right."

"Golly, sweetheart, I just looked at my watch, and it's getting really late for you. And it's a school night too."

"Don't worry. I'll have some strong coffee to wake me up in the morning before class. I'll be just fine."

"Good night, lover. I miss you. And I really am awfully sorry about Valentine's Day."

Matt smiled. "Don't worry about it. We'll both survive. I miss you too. Take care of yourself, and don't you dare fall under the spell of Tyler Jensen." He heard Bradley softly chuckling. "And good night back to you."

Chapter
FOURTEEN

MATT wiped his mouth with a paper napkin that came with his carryout order from Burger King. He wadded up the papers that had wrapped his burger and the little bag that had held his order of fries. Then he stuffed everything into the larger sack that it had all come in when he had walked after his last class to the closest fast food place down the street from the college. Now he wadded it all up into a ball and tossed it into the trash. All that remained was the paper cup with his soft drink, which he had saved to drink while he worked at his desk.

With Bradley so far away in LA, Matt had decided to get his essay papers completed in his office rather than at home. He was tired of dragging work home to an empty apartment because it made him sad whenever he looked up and saw that Bradley wasn't there to distract him from his grading. It was lonely enough without that reminder that he wouldn't be interrupted.

He decided to go to the men's room, almost as a diversion, before he got back to the task at hand. He had given a quiz today and now had two stacks of blue books on his office desk that must be graded in the next few days. Since it was already after 7:00 p.m., there were very few people left in the building. There was one night class down the hall, but it wouldn't let out until around 9:00 p.m. and hadn't gone on break yet. That meant his trip to the men's room was a quick one through the empty hallway. But the men's room was gone when he reached where it usually was. Instead there was a locked janitor's closet. Matt went to the stairs, but they only went up. There were no down stairs.

Rather than go upstairs to search for another men's room, he decided that there was only one thing to do. He went to a trashcan in the hall, fished out an empty paper cup and peed into it, after checking to see that no one else was in the hall. He emptied the cup into a water fountain and shook his head. *What's going on here? Why did I do a thing like that? Where's the damned restroom anyway?* He tossed the empty cup back into the trash.

Matt came back to his office, sat down, and opened the first blue book. He picked up a red pen and just stared straight ahead, rather than at the test booklet. His mind wandered.

Bradley would probably laugh if he knew I miss him bothering me. He smiled and remembered Bradley's impish grin. It made his heart hurt a little.

He looked back at the first test booklet and noticed that the answers were all in French. He slammed it down and picked up another one. It was written in German. *What's happened to my students?*

The phone on his desk rang, startling him. He picked up the receiver.

"Hello?"

There was no answer—just silence on the other end.

"Hello?" Matt repeated. "Is there anyone there? Come on. Speak up if you're there." Only the sound of the dial tone echoed in his ear.

"Maybe it was just a wrong number," Matt said aloud hopefully. He looked at the next test booklet, trying to concentrate. Thankfully it seemed to be in English, but he found that he couldn't read it. It looked like it was written in words and letters, but it made no sense at all. It could have been mathematics equations for all he could tell.

The phone rang again, and it seemed even louder than usual. *Maybe that's because the building is nearly empty,* Matt thought. *Or perhaps it's because it's nighttime. It could be that someone is deliberately trying to drive me crazy.*

"Hello?" Matt said again. He waited, but there was no answer. Then there was a click and the dial tone again. "Damn it," Matt yelled into the phone with no one there. He slammed the receiver down on its base. "I hope it's not the same caller from before who scared me," he said worriedly.

This time Matt made it through about half an hour, the time it took him to grade five test booklets actually written in readable

English, before the phone rang again. He glared at the phone as if he were frozen. It continued to ring, sounding louder in his head each time it rang.

His nerves now thoroughly jarred, Matt picked up the receiver and almost yelled into it. "Hello!"

There was a silent brief pause. "Dr. Sharp? Is that you, Dr. Sharp?"

The voice seemed very familiar to Matt. "Yes. This is Dr. Sharp. Who's calling please?"

The sound of a chuckle came softly from the phone. "It's just me, Dr. Sharp. I saw your lights on in your office, and I thought you might be lonely. Would you like for me to come *join you* while you're *all by yourself, alone, away from everyone* in that cozy little office?" The voice chuckled again ominously.

"What kind of a crazy person are you, anyway?" Matt yelled. "You're just trying to scare me!"

"I tell you what, Dr. Sharp. Why don't you turn off the lights, take off all your clothes, unlock the door, and wait for me to join you? I'll lock the door behind me, strip, and sit with you—*fuck* with you—on that little red sofa by your desk."

Matt screamed and slammed down the receiver once again.

Suddenly the office door began to rattle and shake. Someone was trying to get into the locked office. Matt's nerves finally snapped and he screamed and screamed, over and over again.

His screaming finally woke himself up.

Matt sat up and found that he was in his own bed at home, badly frightened by the terrible nightmare that was too incredibly real. Often Matt was able to tell when he was dreaming even while he was asleep. In whatever dream it was, he would sometimes remind himself that he was merely experiencing a dream. This one had been different. He hadn't been able to tell the difference between reality and the cruel nightmare as it had unfolded.

He knew the recent mysterious call at school and the cryptic note had drastically affected him. *How weird is it that everything seemed so logical and real until that last telephone call?* Matt thought. "I need Bradley," he said out loud, despite himself.

HOURS later Matt sat at the semi-cluttered desk in his university office after the first class of the day. He stared in the general direction of the window, but he didn't really see anything either outside or within his temporary haven from students. He was so deep in thought that the sharp rap on the door startled him.

After taking a few seconds to calm himself, he called out, "Come in. It's not locked."

"Hey there, handsome," a voice replied. "Where have you been keeping yourself today? Besides in class, of course."

Matt breathed a sigh of relief when he realized it was Kristen. He smiled and said, "Hiding out in my little retreat of an office."

"I was looking for you," she said, "because I found a *fabulous* coffee blend at that little place in the Village I told you about last week. You know, the one with some really fine imported blends from all over the world. I brewed a pot this morning and brought you some in this thermos so we could share a comforting cup or two between classes. This one's from Ecuador. Got any paper cups?"

"Aren't you *something*," he said with a grin. "Look over there in that cabinet on the left... top shelf. There's sugar, some sweetener packets, and a container of powdered creamer, if you like. I'll just take mine black."

"Done and done," Kristen replied, doctoring a cup for herself and then pouring out two cups of extremely fragrant and enticing coffee.

"Here you go," she said as she handed him a cup and plopped herself down on the little red leather sofa in front of Matt's desk. "I don't know how you ever got a couch in this tiny office, but it's so much nicer than the old office chairs I've got in *my* office."

"It wasn't easy," Matt replied as he savored the hot coffee.

"I hate to bring up a sore subject, but is there anything new about your mystery note or the weird phone call?"

Matt looked up at Kristen and frowned. "Not exactly. But the whole thing is beginning to have side effects."

"What do you mean?"

"Last night I had a really frightening dream. It was actually more of a combination of what actually happened before with the run-ins I had with that former student, that creepy phone call, and a projection of what my subconscious mind must have invented to happen next. It was troubling how it mixed reality with my fears." Matt then proceeded to tell Kristen his dream.

"Wow. That's really scary all right. I don't blame you for getting frightened by a nightmare like that. Especially when the door rattled and shook. You're right that the note and phone call and all of it together must have caused you to, pardon the pun, dream up the whole thing."

"I think it's pretty clear that's what happened. The weird part was how normal it all was at the beginning with the Burger King stuff and the exams to grade. It was so real that it truly scared me, and the fear lasted for a while even after I woke up."

"Have you actually gotten any more phone calls, visits, or mysterious notes?"

"No. And that's part of the reason I'm upset. Why have only those few incidents made me think that I'm being threatened seriously? I don't think that someone is actually going to kill me. I think a lot of this is just because I miss having Bradley around all the time. He's my security blanket." He laughed. "I just want my Bradley back."

She chuckled. "I get that part, handsome. And I'll agree with you since the note you told me about didn't exactly have a threat. Even the *sour grapes* complaints from that student weren't terribly serious—since you told the dean. And you said the phone call was more or less just a repeat of the note—again, not exactly a threat."

"You think I've let my imagination run away with me?" Matt asked.

Kristin smiled reassuringly. "I think it's possible that, as you already pointed out, your subconscious has run away with you. Of course if anything else happens—especially anything more serious—you definitely need to call campus security again. And perhaps the police too. But I think you need to be patient and just wait to see if anything else comes of it all. At least for the time being. You may not hear another thing about it."

Matt sipped the last of his coffee. "This is exactly why I need you around. You bring me back to earth."

Kristen laughed. "You make it sound like I'm your therapist. If Bradley were here, he'd be telling you the same thing."

"I guess you're right," Matt agreed. "I really think that my missing Bradley so much has put me a little more on edge than I otherwise would be if he were here."

"I think so too. Bradley has more uses than just *one*," she added with a wink and a grin.

At that moment there was another knock on the office door. This time Matt got up to see who was there. To his surprise, Derrick Andrews stood waiting with a man who looked very nearly like him, except he was a few years older. The older man had a firm hold on Derrick's upper arm, almost as if he were trying to keep Derrick from bolting and running down the hall.

"Why, Derrick, I wasn't expecting you today," Matt began. "I have a visitor at the moment...."

Kristen had risen from the sofa and grabbed her thermos. "It's okay, Matt. I need to run along anyway. I believe we've finished our talk for the moment. I'll check with you later this afternoon." She quickly scooted through the doorway and around the two men in the hall.

Derrick looked decidedly uncomfortable, and the other man still firmly held on to him with a tight grip. "Excuse me, Dr. Sharp," the older man said. "I'm Derrick's brother, Daniel Andrews. We need to visit with you, if you can spare a few minutes."

Matt reached out and shook Daniel's proffered hand. "I'm not due in my next class for about an hour so I can spare some time. Come on in." He looked curiously at the hold Daniel had on Derrick as the two men shuffled into the room and seated themselves on the small sofa without being asked.

"What can I do for you?" Matt asked as he settled himself behind his desk.

"It's the other way around, I think," Daniel answered. "Derrick here has something to tell you. Isn't that right, Derrick?"

"I guess so," Derrick mumbled with a frown.

"Well?" Daniel demanded as Derrick lapsed into further silence. "Tell him. You know you have to do it."

Derrick gulped and then looked up into Matt's eyes. "I'm really sorry, Dr. Sharp. I didn't mean any harm. It seemed like a good idea at the time so I just *did it*."

Puzzled, Matt looked intently at Derrick. "Did what?"

"I left that note on your desk. And I called your office extension." Derrick glanced at the phone on Matt's desk.

"*What*?" Matt exclaimed. "That was *you*?"

Derrick shuddered and nearly sobbed as he nodded. "I'm *so sorry*, Dr. Sharp. It didn't dawn on me that I might have scared you until I told Daniel what I did. He explained it to me and made me come here to tell you about it... and apologize."

Matt was almost in shock, and it took him a few moments to respond. Finally he collected his thoughts and cleared his throat. "I sense that there's a story here, Derrick. Let's hear it."

When Derrick remained silent, his brother prodded him with an elbow into his side. "Spill it, Derrick. And start at the beginning."

"Okay, okay," Derrick muttered. "It started several days ago when I followed you and Dr. Spears down the hall after class. I don't know what made me do it, but I eavesdropped and heard you say that your husband was going to be gone to California for a while."

"You make it a habit to *eavesdrop* on your professors?" Matt asked in amazement.

"No. Of course not." Derrick hesitated. "But you're *different*, Dr. Sharp. You're gay. And you're so *cute*."

"That's hardly an excuse."

Derrick swallowed. "I know it. I was just so *attracted* to you. It was not really planned at all. I just saw you two going down the hall that day, and you looked so *serious*. So I followed you and heard what you said. Later, I got to thinking about how lonely you would be with your husband gone. That seemed so sad. Then it dawned on me that you didn't have to be lonely."

"Interesting phrase," Matt said. "You used it in your note *and* on the phone."

"Yes. You see, I went to your office later and found it open. I picked up a scratch piece of paper and jotted down the note to leave for you. I also got your extension number too. That's how I knew how to call you. But I could have looked it up, you know. The campus directory has all the professors' office numbers. Anyway, I wasn't trying to frighten you. I just wanted you to know that I could keep you company and maybe make you smile again."

"Without telling me who you were?"

"Well," Derrick smiled a little for the first time. "It suddenly occurred to me that maybe I had gone too far and I might get into trouble if I told you who I was."

"Very likely," Matt agreed sternly.

"That's why I didn't write or call again. But please, Dr. Sharp. Don't be too angry with me. It was just a dumb, impulsive thing to do. I just went a little crazy for a while. Are you going to have me arrested?"

Matt thought for a moment. "I don't know, Derrick. You really did scare me. Were you ever going to tell me the truth?"

It was Derrick's turn to pause. He looked toward his brother who remained silent. "I'm not really sure. I have to admit that at first it wasn't even my idea to come here today."

"Tell me about it, then," Matt insisted.

"I had too much to drink last night and I told Daniel here what I had done. He was shocked, and I realized too late that I had spilled the beans. Anyway, when I sobered up this morning, Daniel insisted that we come tell you about it. And he was right. It was a really stupid thing to do, and I really *am* sorry." He paused, and then he added, "I also know that I have to face the consequences if you decide to press charges."

Daniel finally spoke up. "Dr. Sharp, Derrick's not really a bad kid. He just made a really bad decision. He's not a very experienced gay man, you know. He just let his feelings get the best of him. I hope you'll take that into consideration while you decide what to do about him."

"Thank you, Daniel," Matt replied. "I will take it all under advisement." He looked at the sorrowful look on Derrick's face. "Don't you remember that we had a discussion a while back about this kind of situation?"

Derrick ducked his head. "I remember...."

"I thought we'd agreed to let it go. And I do recall that you said you had an older gay brother who was quite handsome." He turned to Daniel. "I assume he meant you."

Daniel blushed and nodded. "There are only the two of us."

Matt inwardly debated for a moment more. "All right, Derrick. This business about your attraction to me and your brother's physical appearance is all beside the point. You must put a stop to all this and never make such a mistake again. As for me, I've already found my soul mate, and you need to get busy finding yours. Are we agreed?"

"Oh, yes sir, Dr. Sharp," Derrick exploded. "I promise to never pull a stunt like this again."

Daniel smiled and held out his hand. "You're a generous, kind, and forgiving man, Dr. Sharp. I'm sure Derrick has learned his lesson." He hesitated for a moment. "I'll make sure of that. And by the way, if you weren't already taken, Dr. Sharp...."

Matt grinned despite himself. "Never mind, Daniel. Let's not start that again. Now if you two can find your way out, I need to get ready for my next class." He shook hands with the handsome brothers and sat down briefly as the office door closed.

"Wow," he said to himself. "Who would ever have thought something like that would ever happen to me? But I'm *so glad* that it's over."

THAT evening Matt looked at the clock on the living room wall of the apartment. It was ten thirty. *Hmmm. That means it's seven thirty out west. It's time for a little phone call to the other half.*

He picked up his iPhone from the coffee table and pushed a couple of buttons.

"Hey, sweetie," Bradley chirped. "I'm so glad my honey called."

"Hey back, husband! I have a little story to tell you. No, it's a *big* story. Are you sitting down?"

"I am now," Bradley said. "What's the big story?"

Matt proceeded to relate the events of his remarkable visit from the Andrews brothers.

"Wow. That's kind of a surprise, all right. He seemed liked a nice enough kid when I met him that day in the library—when I was with my weekend hooker."

"Very funny. But I don't care if you joke about it now that this stalker stuff is over at last," Matt said.

"I thought the stalker was going to turn out to be that other student from last year, the one you told me about. What was his name?"

"You mean Gerald Winthrop, the one who threatened me a couple of times. No, that got resolved just a couple of days ago, and I haven't had a chance to tell you about it."

"What happened?"

"It got resolved pretty quickly. The dean and Gerald's father are casual friends. All he had to do was call Gerald and Mr. Winthrop to his office for a little conference," Matt explained. "The dean showed the father Gerald's term paper along with the printed online Wikipedia articles you sent me. Gerald confessed in short order about the cheating and even admitted he threatened me. The dean told me later that Mr. Winthrop was very angry with the kid—and very apologetic about the whole thing."

"Wow again. But I'm a little surprised the dean didn't ask you to be there."

"So was I, when I heard about it, but the dean said he wanted to handle the problem privately with his old friend. I think we've heard the last from Gerald Winthrop."

"Is he going to be punished in any way?" Bradley asked.

"The dean decided to let Gerald graduate—as a favor to Mr. Winthrop—but Gerald has to repeat the course with a different instructor. It will delay his graduation a semester, but I don't care about any of it anymore since it's finally over."

"You've certainly had your share of student issues lately."

"Yes, but I think it'll be a little smoother sailing—for now at least," Matt replied.

"I hope so. You deserve a break."

"So tell me what's new with you—"

Bradley chuckled. "I can't compete with what you've told me."

Chapter **FIFTEEN**

IT HAD been a terribly long day for Matt, and he was convinced that the reason was primarily because of the calendar date. At least that was Matt's excuse for why he was so tired, since it was not only a late Wednesday afternoon but also Valentine's Day. On his way home from school he couldn't help but think about the same thing that had crossed his mind all day—Bradley was in California and they would miss their yearly love celebration for the first time in over eight years. That had made him even more tired and sad.

He had barely closed his apartment door and turned on some lights when a knock sounded at the door. *Maybe it's Bradley after all,* he thought wistfully as he swung the door open again.

"Hi, handsome," a cheery voice cried. "How's tricks?"

Matt almost moaned aloud. "Hi, Clarice. Come on in."

"You don't have to act so *happy* to see me," she retorted with a mock frown. "I've been waiting for you all afternoon."

Matt followed her to the sofa and wearily sat down next to her, really seeing her now for the first time. "How come you're all dressed up like that?"

"I thought you'd *never ask.* And it took you long enough to notice it too. I bought this red dress a couple of weeks ago just to surprise you today."

"What *are* you talking about, Clarice?"

"Well, I'm sure that it didn't escape your notice that today is Valentine's Day. I knew you would mope around all evening because Bradley is gone so I decided to surprise you."

"By dressing up?"

"You are such a drudge. Of course not. I thought it would be good for you to go out tonight for a really classy dinner with me. Maybe that would help cheer you up so you wouldn't just cry over Bradley all evening. What do you think?" She smiled hopefully at him.

Matt sighed. "No, I think I'll pass, Clarice. That's very nice of you to think of me like that, but I'd rather just grab a light snack out of the fridge for dinner and go to bed early. Thanks for being so thoughtful, though."

"Not so fast, mister," Clarice declared. "I don't think I phrased it correctly. You *are* going out to dinner with me tonight. I didn't buy this new dress and make a reservation for dinner *for nothing*, you know. You're going with me whether you want to go or not. Do you understand?" She glared at him as if daring him to refuse.

"That dress looks kind of expensive," Matt said. "Did your mother send you some money again?"

Clarice blushed. "You know very well she did. She likes it that I work in New York, but she knows it's expensive to live here. That's why she gives me an allowance from the trust my father left me. When I reach thirty the trust is mine anyway."

"Sometimes I forget that you're from a family with a lot of money," he replied.

"You're just trying to change the subject. I don't intend to waste this new dress."

Matt grinned. "I'm not going to be able to get out of this, am I? I have a feeling that you would carry me to the elevator and all the way to a cab downstairs if I didn't come with you voluntarily. Isn't that right?"

Clarice laughed. "Well, I'd rather not have to actually *carry you*, but I guess if it really came down to it...."

"All right. I'll make it easy on you and just give up."

"Good. Now you pop in the bedroom and get dressed while I call a cab. There might be a wait this evening because of the holiday so you better get started right now. And wear something nice for the occasion."

Sure enough, they had to stand for several minutes on the sidewalk in front of the building waiting for their cab, but eventually their ride arrived. Clarice opened the cab door first and gave instructions to the driver.

"Where are we going?" Matt asked as he climbed into the taxi. "I couldn't hear what you told him, and you weren't specific when you sprang all of this on me this evening."

Clarice just smiled mysteriously. "It's a surprise so don't spoil it by peppering me with all kinds of questions. You'll enjoy the dinner. I promise you that."

"Okay. I won't ask any more questions."

"Look how heavy the traffic is tonight," Clarice said. "I guess lots of other couples are going out to celebrate just like we are, right in the middle of the week."

"I really wish I had known that you had all of this planned so I could have bought you flowers or a box of candy or something."

"That's very sweet of you," she replied, "but it's totally unnecessary. It's not like we're *that* kind of a couple, after all. But you can do your part by picking up the tab for dinner."

Matt chuckled. "That's what I had in mind."

A few minutes later, the taxi pulled up in front of one of New York's most famous landmarks.

"What are we doing *here* of all places?" Matt asked.

"What's the matter? Don't you like the Empire State Building?"

"Sure. But I thought we were going out to dinner."

"We *are*, silly. I just thought it would be fun to go way up in the sky and have a look at this really romantic city we live in. It will cheer you up when you see all the lights."

Matt climbed out of the cab after paying the cabbie and looked up to the top of the building. "This is very *Sleepless in Seattle* of you, Clarice."

She giggled. "And don't forget *An Affair to Remember*."

"You'd better let me pay for this. I hear it's kind of expensive."

Clarice grinned. "Don't worry about it. I have enough money… but besides that, I have a friend who works here, and he loaned me a pass so we get to go to the top for free. We don't even have to wait in line."

"Of course you do," he replied as he opened the door to the building and led her past the lines and up to the bank of elevators for their ride up to the top. "Why am I not surprised, considering all the friends you have. But I hope you're right about this. Cheering me up, I mean. I can feel a few tears coming because Bradley's not here to share the view... and the moment."

"Now don't start that. I know you miss him, but you've got me and lots of other people around you to keep you company."

As always, it was amazing how quickly the elevator car reached the observation deck. Not too surprisingly, there were already a lot of couples milling around and stopping here and there to gaze at the breathtaking view. Matt and Clarice joined the others, silently absorbing the city for a few minutes.

"I never lose the sense of wonder at the beauty of the city when I come up here," Clarice declared. "It just doesn't ever get old."

He looked at her questioningly. "You come up here often?"

"I've used my friend's pass several times," she informed him.

"Yeah. I feel the same way about this place. It makes a person happy to be in New York." Matt choked up a little at his own words.

Clarice took his arm and snuggled up a little closer to him. "You're so right, honey. But he'll be back in the city before too long. He loves New York just as much as you do. There's even an extra bonus here that's blond and handsome and—"

Matt laughed. But he abruptly stopped laughing as he looked across the crowd of visitors standing with them. He grabbed Clarice's arm tightly. "*Look over there, Clarice.*"

"I see what you mean," she replied. "That woman is wearing a dress almost exactly like mine. The nerve of that store to sell another dress just like this one. They promised me it was an exclusive design and—"

"No, not the *dress*. Look at the man over there in the corner. *It's Bradley!*"

"What? That's not possible," she exclaimed without even looking. "You know as well as I do that he's in Los Angeles this very minute."

"I don't care! *Just look at him!* It's Bradley!"

"No, it's not. He just looks an awful lot like Bradley. Besides, when did you ever see Bradley wearing a *tuxedo*?" She laughed. "And especially at the top of the Empire State Building. This isn't a movie, Matt."

"But it's uncanny. He looks *exactly* like Bradley. I'm going over there to talk to him. I'll prove it to you."

Matt escaped Clarice's clutches and walked up to the man who indeed was wearing a splendid tuxedo. He held a single red rose in one hand while he appeared to be looking for someone in the crowd. "This is just too *Hollywood*," Matt muttered as he neared the stranger who looked so much like his Bradley.

"Excuse me, sir. Don't I know you?" Matt asked.

"I beg your pardon?" a decidedly British accented voice replied. "Were you speaking to me?"

Matt was caught off guard. He examined the man more closely. The hair did seem to be combed a little differently from Bradley's. In the darkness of the night, the man's eyes didn't look exactly like Bradley's green ones either.

"I'm sorry to bother you, but my friend over there and I thought you were someone we know. You look so much like him."

The man gave a small smile. "Oh really? I'm sorry to say that I'm a little suspicious of hearing something like that."

"But it's true. You could be his twin—"

"You must think I'm one of those loony tourists who will fall for anything. I've heard about you New Yorkers—"

"But this isn't a scam. It really isn't," Matt protested.

"Let me guess," the man replied. "You've just flown in from Seattle and you're looking for Meg Ryan up here on Valentine's Day. Don't bother. I've seen the movie."

Matt couldn't help but laugh. "I know it sounds like a ridiculous movie plot, but I really did think you were someone I know. Actually, I thought you were my husband who's supposed to be in California right now."

Now the man gave Matt a closer examination. His attitude seemed to soften a little. "A bit of a poof, are you? Well, you're a good-looking one, I have to say."

Matt blushed at this. "Look, I'm sorry I bothered you. I honestly thought you were someone else, but now I can see the difference." He turned to leave, hiding a sly smile.

"Wait," the stranger called, grabbing Matt's arm. "Don't give up quite so easily. I've often thought about giving it a go with another bloke, but I just never had the chance. Maybe we could go have a shag together someplace. What do you say?"

Matt frowned. "As much fun as that might be," he replied, "I can't do that." He pointed to his wedding ring. "I'm married to a 'bloke' already. And it's quite a remarkable coincidence that he looks an awful lot like you. But that would be just too strange, even if I were willing to cheat on my husband. Of course—he probably deserves it for leaving me all alone in New York." He looked away to keep from laughing and spoiling his joke.

Clarice chose just that moment to approach the two men. "Well, Matt, what did you find out?"

Matt turned to her. "He's British, and he's not nearly as handsome as my Bradley. Actually, now that I look at him more closely, he's not really very good-looking at all. I think it must be the poor lighting up here at night that made me think he looked so familiar."

"Really? You think so?" Clarice asked, staring at the stranger.

"Sure. Look at his hair—it's kind of an ugly cut. And his eyes look sort of shifty and dishonest. They're almost beady and make him look like a criminal or something. Maybe it's even a really ugly woman pretending to be a man."

The man burst out laughing. "Okay, Matt. When did you figure it out? Was it my fake accent?"

Matt smiled. "No, that was actually very good. I liked how you threw in those British words. It sounded quite authentic." He paused. "Want me to tell you what gave you away?"

"I'm dying to hear."

"You're wearing your wedding ring, you goofball. It has the same distinctive design on it as mine, of course." He held up his own ring finger as proof. "See?"

Bradley gulped. "Damn. A little thing like that…."

"What do you mean, *a little thing like that*?" Matt stormed at him.

Now Bradley was laughing again. "*A mere detail*, I meant to say."

"I should have taken you up on your offer of a holiday *shag*. That would have had you going for a while if I had agreed."

"That would have been the end of the game," Bradley replied, not able to hide the smug smile on his face. "There are certain, uh, *details* about a man's anatomy that are pretty unique. Once you had gotten me *uncovered*, shall we say, I think you would have recognized who I was."

"I'm sure you're right about that," Matt agreed. "But I seem to recall a certain Halloween party where Zorro met Robin Hood in the dark and—"

"Never mind. We agreed not to bring that up again."

"Then let's get to the real issue here. How come you're in New York tonight? You said you couldn't come home from LA in the middle of the week."

"Oh, that," Bradley said. "I was just intending to surprise you."

"You did." Matt looked at Clarice who was smiling broadly. "And I suspect you had a little help with this complicated master plan."

"I did indeed. Clarice and I plotted the whole thing out—*just for you.*"

"But wasn't that a little extravagant of you, Clarice, to buy that gorgeous red dress just to lure me up to the top of the Empire State Building on the pretext of dinner?"

Clarice blushed. "I guess it's full disclosure time now. That wasn't completely true. About the dress, I mean. It wasn't just for you. I have a date for dinner tonight as soon as I leave you two lovebirds together." She glanced at her watch. "Actually, I really need to get going so that I can make it to my *real* reservation. Remember Charlie from the library, and from our trip to Atlantic City? He's my dinner date tonight so I have to go."

She gave a quick kiss to Matt and then to Bradley. "It's great to see you again, Bradley, and it's even better to see *Bratt* back together, even if it's just for tonight. See you two later!"

Bradley put his arms around Matt and held him close. "I love you so much. And it's so good to hold you again." Then he gently kissed Matt in front of the lights of New York and everybody.

MATT firmly pressed a dinner napkin to his lips and watched Bradley carefully sip his after-dinner coffee.

"At these prices, I don't want to spill any," Bradley said with a grin. "I'm not complaining about the cost or anything like that, but in my humble opinion, Gaby's is one of the top restaurants in the city, and I want to get my money's worth."

"You couldn't have made a better choice, Bradley. I've wanted to come here for a long time so tonight is just perfect for our first visit. Did you make the reservations, or did Clarice do it for you?"

Bradley laughed. "Reservations at this place are difficult for any weekend, but for Valentine's Day I had to really think far ahead. I had to call early last fall for reservations... before I ever even heard about the firm's new office in LA. That's why I was determined to get back to New York for tonight."

"Did you have any trouble getting off work?"

"Not at all. Winston knows I work for Grace, and he is very accepting of my presence out there. Of course I let him know that besides coming to see you, I wanted to visit with Grace too."

"He probably thought you were going to give her a report about *him*! So he wouldn't object to your trip back to the city in any case."

Bradley grinned. "He is always mindful that I report regularly to Grace. He's not concerned about it because there's nothing to be worried about. He does a great job and we both know it."

"Are you really going to see Grace?"

"She's not back at the office full-time yet, but she's there in the mornings. I thought I'd drop in on her for a little visit in the morning on my way to the airport."

"Good idea. Winston would probably check with her to see if you really did have a conference together."

"That was my thinking too. I really don't have too much to tell her. Things are moving very smoothly at our new offices so I think she'll be pleased and reassured with my little report."

The waiter arrived. "Can I interest you gentlemen in one of our desserts this evening?"

Bradley glanced at Matt who was shaking his head. "I think not. Perhaps another time."

"Then I'll be right back with your check."

Matt looked at his watch. "I know you like to linger over your coffee, but if you have a meeting and a flight to catch in the morning, we'd better head for home."

Bradley feigned a puzzled look. "Whatever makes you think that we're going home, sweetie? We don't have to rush back to the nursing home just yet."

Matt giggled. "But surely you don't intend to take me dancing or something like that when you have to get up so early? And I do have a class in the morning."

"Well, dancing would be nice. That's true. But I have to agree with you that we both have some early-morning responsibilities."

"Then what are you talking about?"

"I just meant that we're not going *home*. We haven't seen each other for six whole weeks, it's a lovers' holiday, and I want something special for us tonight."

"And?"

"And so we are going from here to our reserved suite at the Plaza Hotel."

"The Plaza? Really?"

"Only the best for my husband," Bradley said with a smile.

"Just how much of a salary increase did you get when Grace made you her representative in California?"

Bradley laughed. "Well, we won't go into details at the moment—I'll share that information with you later—but it was enough to allow for a very special evening for the two of us."

"Then I'll let you take care of the check. Here comes the waiter again. I told Clarice that dinner tonight was *on me*, but I believe I'll just let my new British shag partner pay for this one."

The waiter blinked when he overheard Matt's comment, but he said nothing.

"WAKE up, sleepyhead," Bradley urged, gently smoothing Matt's hair out of his eyes as the man struggled to figure out where he was and whether this "Bradley" was just another dream.

"Is that really you?" Matt mumbled. He looked up just as Bradley planted a kiss on his lips. "I didn't think you were real... for a minute, anyway."

"Oh, I'm real all right. And so is the morning. We've got to get moving. There are places that both of us need to be."

Matt smiled. "I don't suppose we have time for just one more go at it before we jump into the shower—together, of course."

"Sadly, the shower is the only thing we have time for right now."

Grumbling, a naked Matt climbed out of bed and followed Bradley's naked body into the bathroom.

A few minutes later as they both stood in front of the hotel, waiting for the doorman to flag a cab for each of them, Bradley leaned over and gave Matt a last kiss.

"I'm sorry, Matt, that this has to be such a short visit, but you'll be out in Hollywood with me during your spring break before you know it."

"Your taxi, sir," the doorman called.

"Be right there." Bradley gave Matt a last hug and hurried to the waiting cab.

"Bye, sweetheart," Matt called, mostly to the empty air since Bradley had already climbed into his cab and slammed the door. He fondled his wedding ring which gave him a little comfort at least.

BRADLEY greeted Marge, who gave him a warm smile and cheery welcome. "I'm popping in to see Grace," he explained as he headed for her office.

"Why, Mr. Moore," she exclaimed. "I didn't realize you were back in town."

"Just for a brief visit. I'm on a flight in a couple of hours back to the other coast. I just thought I'd drop in to see Grace for a few minutes on my way to the airport."

"I'll buzz her to let her know you're here," she replied.

Bradley knocked quietly on the door to Grace's inner sanctum and was pleased by the wide smile on her face as she rose to greet him.

"Welcome back, Hollywood," she said. "Why didn't you let me know you were coming?"

"Well, I was only in town overnight, but I wanted to drop by for a quick hello."

Grace eyed him shrewdly. "I'm not surprised that you're here, you know. After all, yesterday was Valentine's Day. I just bet you had an intimate reunion with your other half."

Bradley grinned back at her. "How right you are. Winston didn't seem to mind my being gone for a couple of days. He just assumed I was coming to see you. In some ways, I try to defer to him, only as a courtesy of course."

"Yes, I know. And he wasted no time calling me to say you were on your way." Grace laughed. "I think you still make Winston a little nervous, Bradley. And I'm glad you're keeping him on his toes."

"Oh, he has no reason to be anxious about anything. I think he's doing a terrific job out there with the new branch firm. You'd approve of the way he's handling things, I'm sure."

"Just the same, I'm glad you're out there to offer input on my behalf. By the way, I was pleased that none of you had any trouble passing the bar exam in California."

"We studied," Bradley replied with a grin. "You knew we wouldn't let you down."

"I'm well aware of it."

"You look marvelous. How do you feel now that you're back at work part-time?"

"I'm getting stronger every day. My doctor is going to let me come back full time in about three weeks, he said. I'm working my way up to it by stages."

"I'm very relieved that you're doing so well."

"So am I. Well, is there anything new to report?" she asked as he sat down in front of her.

"Not really. I've put just about everything in those reports I've been sending you each week."

"A courtesy call? I appreciate that, Bradley, and I look forward to your permanent return in a couple of months. You *do* plan to return, don't you?"

"You surprise me, Grace. Whatever makes you ask that?"

Grace smiled. "I'm in touch with Winston very often too. I got the impression from him that you've been surprised at how much you enjoy being in Los Angeles. Are you thinking of staying out there with Winston?"

Bradley hesitated just a moment too long so Grace silently stared at him. "I have to admit something to you, Grace," he finally said. "It's not like I had expected it to be at all. I thought I'd be bored to tears and pine away for New York every minute. But surprisingly, I've discovered that I like the West a lot more than I would have dreamed. In all honesty, it *has* crossed my mind a few times to ask Winston if he'd like for me to stay and to ask Matt if he could ever consider a move to California."

Now it was Grace's turn to hesitate. "Do you really think you might want to stay out there?" she asked. "You're one of my favorites, you know, but I wouldn't stand in your way if that's what you really wanted to do. I wouldn't like it—not for a moment—but I wouldn't stop you, Bradley. As a matter of fact, you could continue to be my 'eyes and ears', so to speak, and report back to keep me informed about things out there."

"I really can't answer you just yet. I've only been gone for about six weeks so it's a little early for me to make such a major decision like that. Besides, Matt gets the most major consideration in my life. That's no surprise to you."

"I know that, Bradley, and I completely understand. I just ask that you keep me informed about your thinking. I'd rather have you here, but we'll just see how things go for you out there."

"Thanks, Grace. I really do appreciate all you've done for me." He looked at his watch. "I think I'm going to have to go hail a cab if I'm going to make my flight. There's no point in making Winston sweat it out by thinking we're having a huge powwow over him. I assume you got my latest report in the e-mail I sent before I left LA."

"Of course. Thanks for keeping me informed. It's been wonderful to see you, Bradley." Grace rose from her desk. "Continue to keep me posted—on everything."

"I will. Goodbye, Grace."

Chapter SIXTEEN

BRADLEY reached to answer the ringing telephone on his desk.

"Mr. Moore, you have a visitor. Mr. Tyler Jensen is here to see you."

"Thanks, Janet. Send him right in, please."

Bradley rose as Tyler entered his office and quietly closed the door behind him. He offered his hand and said, "Hey there, Tyler. It's good to see you again. Sit down, won't you?"

Tyler shook Bradley's hand, a little more warmly and intimately than most of Bradley's visitors would, and Bradley smiled gently at his famous friend.

"I appreciate your seeing me without an appointment," Tyler began, "but since I was already here for a conference, I thought I'd drop in to say hello."

"You're welcome anytime, Tyler. I take it that you were here to see Winston. How's it going with the contract dispute?"

Tyler laughed softly. "It couldn't have gone better. Everything's signed and sealed, though not delivered quite yet. Your Mr. Kirby is quite good at what he does."

Bradley nodded in agreement. "That's why he's the head of our West Coast offices."

"When the negotiations began on my contract with the network, I think their attorneys thought they were in for an easy time of it. McKenna, Kirby, and Associates is brand new in LA, after all. I guess the network thought they were dealing with novices." Tyler laughed. "They either forgot or didn't know that they were up against a high-powered, seasoned New York attorney."

Bradley laughed too. "That's right. Winston's been around the block before with East Coast show business attorneys. He's got an excellent reputation for being tough. I'm surprised your network didn't do some research on him."

"Well, anyway," Tyler continued, "Winston got me a nice raise for next season and an extension of my contract so I couldn't be more pleased."

"I'm glad to hear it, but I'm not at all surprised."

"However, I stopped in to see you for a different reason."

"Oh? How can I help you?" Bradley asked.

"This is a social matter rather than a business one," Tyler explained. "I realize this is extremely short notice, but I wanted to ask you out for tonight."

Bradley grinned. "You mean an evening of barhopping or something like you mentioned before? To some out-of-the-way places?"

Tyler grinned slyly. "Maybe another time. I had something else in mind for tonight."

Now Bradley smiled affectionately. "If you mean a real date, you know that I'm married to Matt."

"We've been through all that," Tyler interrupted and smiled back. "I'm merely inviting you to a dinner party in Beverly Hills at a good friend's house. It's not at all a *date*."

"Hmmm. I actually don't have any dinner plans for the evening. And I'm getting kind of tired of going to one restaurant after another with Elliot. Nothing against Elliot, of course. He *is* my best friend."

"Maybe your best friend might like the chance to be on his own and do a little barhopping or partying without you. I'm sure it's hard to make *connections* with a *buddy* around all the time."

Bradley laughed. "You're right about that, I'm sure. He hasn't complained, but I bet he might like the chance to do a little exploring on his own."

"So is it a date? Uh... I mean an *appointment*?" Tyler chuckled.

"You talked me into it," Bradley replied. "It'll be nice to do something a little different."

"There's one more thing," Tyler added. "It's somewhat formal so you need to dress up a bit."

"Do I need to rent a *tux*?"

Tyler laughed. "No. We're not going to the Academy Awards or to the Emmys. Just don't wear shorts and a T-shirt. A business suit will do nicely."

"But I thought that California casual was all the rage," Bradley said dryly.

"That's right, but we're not going to the beach or shopping at a mall, either. Come to think of it, if you were to wear just a bikini swim suit, you'd make a big *splash* and a lot of new *friends*."

Bradley raised his eyebrows. "What kind of party *is* this, anyway?"

"I was just teasing you. We're going to a very quiet dinner with some gay friends of mine who like to observe a few formalities once in a while. If we went there tomorrow night, for example, it might be perfectly all right to wear swimsuits. He might be giving a swim party in that big pool he's got in the backyard. Who knows?"

"I get it. I'll dress appropriately. What's the address?"

"Actually, I thought I might just drop by your place and pick you up," Tyler replied.

"I don't mean to be ungrateful, but what if I want to leave before you're ready to go? Would I take a taxi or something?"

Tyler laughed again. "Bradley, we're not going to a fraternity beer bust or to an orgy! It's just a little pleasant dinner with a drink or two afterwards. All of us, and I do mean *all of us*, have to go to work early in the morning. The studios expect us to report very early for makeup and wardrobe."

"So these friends of yours are actors?"

"Of course. Most of my friends are in the business. Anyway, you don't need to worry about being out too late. None of us can afford to do that. We'll leave as soon as you're ready. You might even want to stay *later* than I do. Who knows?"

Bradley pointed to the wedding ring on his left hand. "I doubt that very seriously."

"Back to business, then. Where do you live so I can pick you up?"

"Here... I'll just jot down the address of the apartment complex." Bradley began writing on one of his business cards. "And here's my phone number too. Just call me when you arrive, and I'll come out to the parking lot so you don't have to search for the apartment."

"Okay, but are you afraid for me to see which apartment is yours?"

Bradley chuckled. "Not at all. I'll show you which one it is later, if you like. I'm just trying to save you some time and trouble."

Tyler took the card, glanced at it, and put it into his pocket. "I know where this is. I'll be there about seven thirty. See you then."

"Fine. See you later. And thanks for the invitation. I'm looking forward to the evening already." Bradley stood as Tyler rose to leave.

"So am I. Until later, then."

MATT was sitting in his office correcting hour quizzes when his iPhone signaled an incoming call. He smiled when he saw that it was Bradley calling.

"Hello, lover. How's everything in California?"

"I'd love to be with you right now to tell you all about it. I can't wait until you're here in a couple of weeks," Bradley replied. "But everything is fine. And I can't tell you how great it was to be with you on Valentine's Day—and the night too, of course."

"It was the best Valentine's we've ever had," Matt replied. "Maybe that's because we'd been apart for a while."

"Or maybe it's because you've always fancied a shag with a British gent," Bradley said in his fake accent again. "I'm ready for a do-over whenever you're ready, you adorable little wanker."

Matt laughed. "Come and get me."

"By the way, I meant to ask you something when I was in New York. Are you feeling better now the big mystery with Derrick is over?"

Matt let out a long breath. "You bet. It's such a relief not to worry about that anymore. I've been spending time thinking about my LA trip instead of dreading notes and phone calls."

"Good. I'm so glad. I guess you've got your airline tickets and boarding passes already."

"Sure do. It's all taken care of. I've even got some stuff packed and ready to go. It *is* nice and warm out there this time of the year, isn't it?"

Bradley laughed. "It's almost *always* nice and warm out here... just about *all* times of the year."

"That's really different from here in New York, as I'm sure you remember. Anyway, the reason I asked is because most of the things I've packed are for warm weather."

"Then you're all set. However, something was brought to my attention this morning which I was going to mention to you anyway. It's one of the reasons I called."

"What's that?"

"Just in case, I think you might want to pack at least one lightweight business suit. We might go to some fancy restaurant or even to a formal party. California is mostly casual all right, but there are a few times when you might need something a little dressier."

"Okay, but what did you mean that it was brought to your attention this morning?"

"That's what I was going to tell you about. I have a *date* this evening, and I have to wear a business suit."

Matt paused for a moment. "What do you mean you have a date this evening? A business dinner or something?"

Bradley laughed again. "I'm sorry I was so mysterious... and so misleading. It's not really a date, and it's not business either. Remember what I told you about Tyler Jensen?"

Matt's voice was a little cooler this time. "Yes, I remember. You're going out with *him*?"

"Now don't get jealous, sweetie. It's just a dinner party at some friend's house in Beverly Hills."

"You have friends in Beverly Hills now?"

"I can tell that you're taking this *far* too seriously. No, I don't have friends out here at all. Tyler is just a client and a slight acquaintance. He stopped by this morning after his visit with Winston and asked me to dinner. It's nothing serious. I was thinking that after I meet his Beverly Hills actor friend, maybe I could get an invitation for you and me to his house when you get here. I thought you might like to meet a star or two."

"Besides Tyler?"

"Sure. You can meet Tyler, but I hope you can meet some others too."

"Whose house is this, anyway?"

"I actually forgot to even ask. I'm assuming it's some Hollywood star and his friends who are still in the closet. But don't you think it would be fun to meet some stars?"

Again Matt hesitated for a moment. "Yes, you're right. It *would* be fun. I just didn't want you to get *too* chummy with Tyler and his friends. He *is* pretty good-looking, you know."

"I hadn't noticed."

"I'm *sure*."

"No. Really. You're the only one for me and you know it. Besides, I always point out my wedding ring and love to show your photo that I keep in my wallet."

Matt chuckled. "Glad to hear it, sweetheart. I really do miss you *so much*."

"And I miss you too. Are you still at the university this afternoon?"

After a sigh, Matt replied. "Yes. I'm stuck here for a while grading papers."

"Well, I guess I'd better let you get back to it. I wouldn't want to think of you still slaving away at school this evening while I'm out to a fancy dinner."

"Ha ha," Matt said dryly. "But you're right. I'd better get this done. Thanks for calling, and I love you."

"I love you too. Can't wait to see you again."

MATT only had time to grade one more paper before a knock sounded on his office door. "Come in," he called, setting down his grading pen on the next paper awaiting his attention.

"Hi, Matt," Kristen greeted him. She held the door open for a stranger Matt did not recognize. "I hate to interrupt you, but I wanted you to meet someone."

Matt looked up at the stunning young man who entered the office with Kristen. His heart picked up its pace a little as he tried not to stare too openly at the gorgeous man who held out his hand.

"Matt, this is David Strasser. He's a strong candidate for a position in the English department. He and I took some graduate classes together a few years ago at NYU when we were both getting our doctorates so he stopped by to see me after his interview with the English chair."

"I'm so happy to meet you, Dr. Sharp. Kristen has said so many nice things about you."

Matt smiled warmly and reached to shake hands and gesture for the two to sit down on the sofa. "I'm pleased to meet you too, Dr. Strasser."

"Oh, you two are being too formal. Matt, this is David. David, he's Matt. I bet that you're both probably about the same age too."

They smiled at each other, and Matt thought, *I wonder if he's gay.*

"David tells me his interview went extremely well, and the chairman gave him a hint he might be offered the position very shortly."

"How wonderful." Matt exclaimed. "Then I look forward to getting to know you better."

David smiled broadly and gave Matt an almost imperceptible little wink. "And I'm excited about meeting possible new colleagues too. I haven't lived in New York for a few years so I don't really know many people anymore. I hope we can become friends."

Matt grinned. "I hope so too," he replied.

A cell phone sounded and interrupted any reply David might have made.

"Oh, that's mine," Kristen announced. "It's my 'gentleman caller', so I'd better take the call." She grinned at their surprised expressions. "He's Southern so I call him that for fun. Excuse me for a moment." She stepped outside the office, leaving Matt and David alone as she closed the door.

Matt cleared his throat and looked at David. "So, David, where have you lived since you were at NYC for your graduate studies?"

David grinned. "Really far away. I've been all the way over in Connecticut. But let's skip over the chitchat, shall we? You're gay, aren't you? And don't look so *stunned*—I'm gay too. That's why I'm so happy to make your acquaintance. I like having gay friends who are also professionals."

Matt studied David for a moment. "Well, I guess I'm glad that you're so up front about it. So am I. *Gay*, that is, and fairly open about it too. Although I'm certainly not hiding in the closet, I don't go around advertising it to just everyone."

"I think it's a good thing we got the basics over with." David said, smiling. "We won't have to play guessing games now, and it's a start if we're going to be on staff together. And, of course, that's still just an 'if'."

"I hope that it works out for you—"

Kristen came back into the office with a smile. "We're going out for a special dinner tonight, sort of a special private celebration. What did I miss?"

"Just some gay chatter between new friends," Matt replied.

"Kristen didn't tell me about you, I hope you understand that," David insisted. "You know she wouldn't break a confidence. I just hoped you were gay when I saw you and decided to ask."

Kristin turned to Matt. "I just thought it would be nice if you two met, in case David joins our staff."

"I agree," Matt said. "The 'new guy' always needs a friend. David is lucky enough to have two of us right off the bat."

Now Kristen looked from Matt to David and back again to Matt. "Maybe it's a good time for me to ask about Bradley. How is he doing these days?"

"Who's Bradley?"

"I didn't get a chance to tell him," Matt replied. "Bradley is my husband. He's in Los Angeles for a few months working to establish his law firm's new branch office. Let me show you his picture."

Matt turned on his phone and pulled up two candid snapshots he had taken during the Christmas holidays. "Here's Bradley."

It was barely noticeable, but Matt saw the slight disappointment on David's face.

David forced a smile. "He's a real keeper, all right. I bet you really miss him while he's all the way out there in California."

"Oh, I do. But he was here for Valentine's Day, and I'm going out there soon for spring break."

"That's really nice," David said without much enthusiasm as he handed the phone back to Matt.

"I hate to break this up," Kristen announced, "but I really must go."

"So do I," David added. "I've got quite a way to go to get home. It was nice to see you again, Kristen. And I enjoyed meeting you, Matt."

"It was my pleasure. I'm stuck here doing some grading so I guess I'd better get back to it."

Kristen hugged both men and left as Matt shook David's hand on his way out of the office.

"COME on out, I'm waiting for you," Tyler sang out on his cell phone.

"Be right there," Bradley replied and then clicked off his phone. He turned to his roommate. "So what do you have going for tonight, Elliot?"

Elliot smiled broadly. "Since you're going to the private gay boys' dinner party tonight and I don't have to babysit you, I'm going to take our friend Tyler's suggestion and go barhopping. I'm glad Tyler's picking you up so I can have our rental car for the evening."

"It would have been wasteful for both of us to rent a car when we usually just go to work together anyway."

"Speaking of cars, I'm thinking of looking for one of my own this weekend now that I'm living in LA. It just wasn't practical to have one in New York."

"Maybe I could go with you. I think I'd like to look around at new car showrooms, just for fun."

"Okay. Does that mean you're thinking of buying a car too? And maybe staying out here in LA after all?"

"Elliot, we've already been through all that. I just thought it would be fun to go with you since I don't own one."

"Fine. I'll enjoy the company, but for now you'd better get going. Your movie star date might be getting *impatient*."

"I told you, it's not a *date*, and he's a TV star, not a movie star."

"Whatever... but he's still out there waiting."

"See you later, Elliot. Don't wait up." Bradley laughed as he breezed out the apartment door.

Elliot grinned. "As if I would."

When Bradley walked toward the parking lot, he hardly expected the sight that awaited him. Tyler, wearing dark shades, a huge grin, and a handsome dark-gray suit, stood leaning against a bright-red sports car convertible.

Bradley's eyes nearly popped as he stared at the open scissors doors of the Lamborghini parked in front of him.

Tyler smiled even more broadly and waved casually. "Hey, Cinderella! Your coach is ready to take you to the ball."

"I can hardly believe *this car*," Bradley gasped. "What exactly *is* it?"

Tyler giggled. "It's my one and only real splurge since I got my network TV series and the salary that goes with it. To be specific, it's a Lamborghini Murciélago LP640 Roadster. Do you like it?"

Bradley laughed. "I *love* it, but I don't even know how to *get into it*."

"Just slide into the front seat. I'll close the doors and take care of the rest."

Bradley did as he was told, and Tyler carefully edged the car out of the parking lot and into the stream of traffic as they began speeding toward Beverly Hills.

"You took my breath away this time, Tyler. But you really didn't have to buy me such an expensive 'Welcome to LA' gift. The invitation to a dinner party was enough."

Tyler laughed. "I like you, Bradley, but I'm *not* giving you my car."

"By the way, I forgot to ask you this morning where we're going tonight. Who's giving the dinner party?"

"Didn't I mention it? It's a friend of mine who also has his own TV series. Maybe you've seen his show, *Danger Drives Me*."

"You mean Cole Bristow? Really? That's the show about the ex-racecar driver turned private detective who goes around solving crimes in LA, right? I've seen it a few times, but Matt is a devoted fan."

"Cole and I met when I first came to town from Seattle. He was just getting started too, and we went to some of the same casting calls. We ran into each other so many times that we eventually became friends."

"Wow. It'll be fun meeting him and telling Matt about it later. And I'm actually going to his *house* too."

"Well, don't get *too* star struck over it. He's just a regular guy, and a pretty nice one too. Now this is just between us, you understand, but he and I dated for a while a few years ago."

"That's pretty exciting. But you're not a couple now?" Bradley asked.

"No. It just wasn't meant to be. We weren't exactly right for each other... but we're very good friends. By the way, I know that I don't need to tell you this about attorney-client privilege, but the gay men you'll meet tonight *do not* broadcast their orientation. This is all confidential."

"Of course, Tyler. I understood that from the very beginning."

"Good. I just needed to mention it."

Bradley looked at the mansions as they cruised through Beverly Hills. "Some of these places look more like palaces than homes."

Tyler grinned. "That's right, but Cole's place is one of the more modest ones. You might be surprised to learn there are a number of 'mansions' in this area that are valued at less than a million dollars. I know because I looked up the prices of some mansions online."

Bradley laughed. "What about Cole's house?"

Tyler looked a little sheepish. "I looked it up too. It's valued around two million. But that's still on the low end compared to the really expensive twenty-five to over one hundred million dollar showplaces around here."

"Okay. I'm officially impressed with the property values in this neighborhood."

"We're just about there," Tyler announced as he pulled into the circular driveway of an attractive, but not particularly elaborate, two-story house. It was beautifully landscaped and quite welcoming. There were four or five expensive-looking cars already parked in the spacious, mostly hidden off-the-street parking area near the entrance to the house.

Tyler parked his car near the others and led Bradley to the front door where a handsome butler, at least Bradley assumed that he was a butler, took the two men into a stylishly appointed living room. It was easily larger than Bradley and Matt's entire New York apartment.

"Don't be *too* overly impressed," Tyler whispered in warning. "You'll sound like an eager autograph-seeking fan. That's not something you want to be."

"I'll be careful," Bradley said, smiling.

"Hello, Tyler, you good-looking hunk," greeted a handsome dark-haired man with piercing green eyes. He hugged Tyler, gave him a quick kiss on the lips, and stood back to gaze at him. Then his eyes turned to examine Bradley. He stared for a moment. "So this is our newest guest?"

"Cole, I'd like to introduce one of my attorneys, Bradley Moore. He's with the firm that settled my contract dispute with the network."

Cole's smile became somewhat artificial. "Your attorney?"

"Well, yes. But he's a new friend too." Tyler grinned. "Oh, and there's one other thing, Cole," he added as he planted a quick kiss on Bradley's cheek, "he's *one of us*."

Now Cole laughed out loud. "I understand at last. I wondered why you'd bring your attorney to dinner... even though he is an awfully cute one."

Bradley blushed. "That's the strangest introduction I've ever had."

"I didn't mean to make it so awkward. I apologize," Cole said. "But let me introduce the other dinner guests." He led Bradley into the room where four men and a woman were sitting on various chairs and settees, sipping what looked like martinis.

"First, I'd like you to meet Arthur Conley, then Glen Larson, Mel Richards, and Ronald Whiting." Cole winked at Bradley and added, "I'm sure they hope you've seen each of them before—most likely on your television screen at home."

Bradley shook hands with each one in turn and smiled broadly because he did indeed recognize them all from various TV programs he'd seen over the past few years.

"I'm a fan of them all," Bradley said to Cole. At a warning look from Tyler, he added, "but I'm not a stalker or autograph hunter, I assure you."

They all chuckled and murmured their welcomes to Bradley.

"I've left the lady for last, Bradley. I'd like you to meet Alice Grant."

Bradley shook her proffered hand too, and noted that Alice gazed at him with a definite look of interest.

She gave him a grin. "I'm sure you wonder what I'm doing here in this gay men's gathering. I'm Cole's agent."

"And she's an indispensable one too," Cole quickly pointed out. "I don't know what I'd do without her. And as Tyler explained about *you*, Alice is a friend as well as an agent."

Bradley smiled and relaxed a bit as he glanced about at the various guests.

"I'd ask you to sit down and join us, and I'd offer you a cocktail—but I actually had something else in mind first. I *will* offer you a drink later, but I thought it would be fun if we all had a brief swim before dinner."

Startled, Bradley looked to Tyler who was grinning at him. "Why did we have to dress up if we're going swimming?" he said softly. "And I didn't bring a swimsuit."

Cole had stepped closer and happened to overhear Bradley's remarks. "Don't worry, Bradley. It's a common event before dinner at my house. They've all stashed swimsuits here for times like this—even Alice has got one."

"But I don't..." Bradley stammered.

Cole's eyes moved slowly up and down Bradley's body. "If I'm not mistaken, you probably wear the same size I do, and I've certainly got an extra suit for you. I'll run upstairs and get one, and then we can all get dressed in the cabana out back by the pool."

Looking at Bradley's uneasy expression he said, "We'll *take turns* changing in the cabana. No one's going to... uh... make embarrassing plays for your favors." He laughed. "And yes, I noticed your wedding ring right away. You won't get cruised or approached in any way."

Again Bradley blushed. "I didn't mean to imply that—"

"Bradley," Cole interrupted. "Don't worry about it. This isn't a gay bathhouse." He laughed. "We're all just friends here for a pleasant evening. We want you to have a relaxing good time."

"Of course," Bradley agreed. "I know that, but LA is still a new place for me, and I certainly don't know my way around socially in Beverly Hills. I just didn't know quite what to expect."

Cole smiled as Tyler joined them. "Let's go out back and have a refreshing swim before dinner. Tyler will show you the way, and I'll see about that swimsuit for you."

"You could have warned me about this," Bradley began after Cole had left.

"And miss the look of horror and surprise on your face? Never." Tyler laughed and led the way.

SWIMMING sessions in Cole's pool before dinner were usually short but exhilarating, and that was the case this evening as well. By the time the spirited horseplay in the pool had ended, Bradley didn't feel as self-conscious about showering and dressing for dinner in front of Tyler's and Cole's gay friends in the spacious cabana. A feeling of camaraderie had begun in the little group by the time they sat down to the scrumptious dinner in the formal dining room.

Cole glanced around the table set for eight. "My friends who've dined here before, Bradley, know that my intent in enjoying the pool first is to bring people together who might not know each other very well and to build an appetite. I hope that's worked tonight."

"I think you succeeded," Tyler replied. "Of course, I already know everyone here, but Bradley as the newcomer seemed to fit right in."

"That's right," Ronald agreed. He turned to Bradley. "Are you a permanent resident in LA now?"

Bradley shook his head. "Sadly, I'm not. Our firm is trying to establish itself on the West Coast, and I'm just here to help get it started. I'll be going back to New York soon."

"Speaking for all the others," Mel injected, "I'll tell you that we've all noticed that ring on your finger. I imagine therein lies a story."

Bradley grinned and glanced at the ring. "I'm married to a wonderful man. He's a history professor at a small college in New York." He pulled out his wallet, removed Matt's photo, and passed it around the table, to a chorus of approvals. "Ironically, we got married here in California during that brief period before the notorious Proposition 8 was passed. But we didn't live here. We were just visiting at the time."

Cole set his cutlery down on his plate and looked directly at Bradley. "Have you ever thought about a career in show business?"

Bradley laughed. "Not really. My experience in public performance is limited to the courtrooms of New York City." He chuckled. "Why do you ask?"

Cole hesitated. "I've been studying you since you arrived."

The others laughed and groaned at the same time. Then grins appeared on all their faces except Bradley's and Alice's.

"That's a very tired old pick-up line," Glen said with a smirk. "Are you going to offer him a part in your TV series next? And then are you going to offer your services as a close personal advisor?"

Again the others laughed, but Cole joined in this time. Only Alice looked thoughtful.

"All right, Glen. I know Bradley's already taken, but I was being halfway serious... sort of."

"What?" Bradley asked. "But I'm not an actor. I'm an attorney."

"I know that," Cole replied, "and I'm not trying to engineer a career change for you. But I was thinking about the script for my next show. There's a tiny part at the very beginning of the episode that might be perfect for a good-looking man like you."

"You can't be serious," Bradley argued. "I don't have any experience in acting... or any interest in it, either."

"Look. I know you're not an actor. I know you won't be here for long. But there's this part that you could do, and it would just be for fun. Something to tell your husband about, and something for your

New York friends to enjoy when it's aired in May. Don't tell me you wouldn't enjoy a one-day experience being in a TV show."

"Something like that never occurred to me," Bradley said.

"Isn't a courtroom appearance like a performance? It's just another form of acting," Cole continued. "I'm just saying that as soon as I saw you, I thought of this little part. It would just be for a lark and, as I said, for fun. Certainly not for the money—it would be union scale."

"You really might have a good time," Tyler interjected. "Why don't you think about it?"

Cole persisted. "Let me just tell you the essence of the scene so you can consider this seriously."

Bradley looked skeptical. "Okay. I guess that would be all right."

"It takes place at the very beginning before the credits of the show. There's a shot of an accounting firm's office in a large building. It's night, and one of the accountants, that would be you, sits working at this desk. Only a few lights are still on in the office. The buzzer sounds on the desk, and the secretary asks to go home for the night. The accountant asks the secretary to come in first. He looks up when the secretary comes to his desk. The secretary says something like 'Is that all for today?', and the accountant stands up and kisses the secretary. He says something like 'That's all... until we get to *your place*. I'll just be a little bit longer. Wait for me....' The secretary leaves, and the accountant begins to wrap up his work. Suddenly, a shadow appears. The accountant looks up. We see a gun, and the gun fires. The accountant falls forward onto his desk, dead."

"That sounds pretty good," Tyler said. "It's short but not exactly sweet." He laughed.

"That's all there is to it?" Bradley asked. "I'd just have to kiss the secretary and fall over dead when I'm shot?"

"That's it," Cole replied. "Then I spend the rest of the episode trying to find out who killed you and why they did it. Sound like fun?"

Bradley was quiet for a moment. "It doesn't sound all that bad," he admitted. "Your show is one of my husband's favorites. I bet he'd get a kick out of seeing me on it."

Cole nodded. "I bet he would. So you'll do it?"

"Let me talk to Matt first. Can I let you know tomorrow?" Bradley asked.

"I hate to burst everyone's bubble," Arthur said, speaking up for the first time. "But is it legal for a non-professional like Bradley to take a role in a TV show?"

"Oh, that's right," Tyler said. "He doesn't have a membership in SAG."

"Are they that strict for just a bit part like this?" Bradley asked.

"The Screen Actors Guild is pretty powerful and strict too. You're supposed to have a card, or membership, in SAG in order to be in any TV show," Cole added.

Alice finally spoke up. "I've been studying Bradley too, and had almost the same thought as Cole did about putting him in a small role. I could serve as his temporary agent and I can tell you that there are ways to get around SAG. For one thing, if there are enough SAG members in the cast, it's all right to use a non-union actor in a small part like this. Or if there isn't a SAG member available, you can do it. I bet either case could apply on your show, Cole. I'll look into it with the producer and the director first thing tomorrow."

"I really appreciate that you would go to bat for me, Alice, but I still ought to talk to Matt about this first."

"Well, let's just leave it at that," Cole said. "Alice can check on the possibility of using you in the show, and Bradley can check with Matt. We'll confer on this tomorrow. Are we agreed?"

Bradley and Alice nodded, and the others all smiled.

"This would be *just for fun*," Bradley repeated. "Just a *one-time deal*."

Everyone nodded.

The smile on Bradley's face grew bigger as the dinner ended and a final glass of port was served to the guests. *Wait until I tell Matt about all this....*

MATT'S phone abruptly sounded and woke him up at one in the morning. He reached for it and saw that Bradley was calling.

"Hi, sweetheart. Is everything all right?"

"Oh, sure," Bradley replied. "I just needed to tell you about the party in Beverly Hills tonight where I went with Tyler Jensen."

"I'm really happy to hear from you, Bradley," Matt replied, "but did you really call me in the middle of the night to talk about a *party*? Wait a minute. What do you mean that you *need* to tell me about it? Did something happen?"

"Well, yes. For one thing we had a swimming party first—before dinner, I mean."

"You were all dressed up and had to change to a swimsuit before dinner? That's odd."

"Not as odd as it seems at first, you see—"

"Never mind all that. Get to the story. Did someone try to get inside your swimsuit or take it off of you in the pool?"

Bradley laughed. "Nothing as serious as all that. They were all really nice guys. You would know who they are too. There're all TV stars. There was Mel Richards and Glen Larson—"

"Would you cut out all the name dropping and get to the point?" Matt snapped. "You're making me worry."

"Sorry, sweetie. I just thought you'd like to know all the stars I met at the party," Bradley explained.

"And you're right. I would like to hear all about it, but not so much in the middle of the night. After class tomorrow—later today, I mean—would be better."

Bradley sighed. "Okay. I'll get to the point. The party was at Cole Bristow's house."

"The star of *Danger Drives Me*? Oh, I just love that show."

"Well, anyway, Cole wants me to be in an episode of it."

"*What?* He wants *you* to be on *Danger Drives Me*? I can't believe it."

"It's only a tiny part at the very beginning of the episode. I would play a character who gets murdered in the first scene. The rest of the plot would be about solving my murder."

"Wow. How did this happen? You're not an actor."

"Cole just said he thought I looked perfect for the part. His agent is going to check whether SAG would let me be in the show as a non-professional."

"What's that?" Matt asked.

"Oh, that stands for Screen Actors Guild, and they have rules for—"

"Don't be such a know-it-all, Bradley. Agent? What's going on?"

"Cole's agent was at the dinner, and she said she'd talk to the producer and director to see if they'd let me play the part. That's all. It would be a one-day job, and I'd only get paid union scale. I would only do it for the fun of it, and if *you* thought it would be all right."

"You told them that? That you wanted *my approval*?"

"I did," Bradley said. "I won't do it if you don't want me to."

"You're not thinking of becoming a Hollywood actor, are you?"

"Of course not. I told you it would just be for fun, and it would be because I know you *like* that show. I thought you might enjoy seeing me in it—this one time, anyway."

Matt laughed. "I don't especially want to see you get murdered, but it *would* be fun to see you in a little scene. But why did you call about all this at such a late hour?"

"I had to, honey. They need to know early tomorrow if I can shoot my scene one day next week. If you say it's okay, they'll send me a script."

"Now that I'm fully awake, I think it sounds like a lot of fun. Of course you must do it, if they give approval. *Tell them you'll do it.*"

"You're sure?" Bradley asked.

"I'm sure. When will the episode be on TV?"

"Cole said it would be sometime in May. By the way, at dinner tonight they all asked about my ring so I showed your photo to everyone. They liked how you look."

"You're so sweet. I love you so much, and I can't wait to get out there to see you."

"I love you too. And I may have some surprises for you when you get here."

"That reminds me. I have a little something to tell you in the way of news."

"Oh? What's that?"

"I met a potential new faculty member this afternoon. He's an old friend of Kristen's, and she brought him to meet me in my office."

"That's nice, I guess."

"I haven't told you the good part. He's extremely handsome and very friendly."

Bradley was silent for a moment. "Okay. Let's hear the rest of it."

Matt chuckled. "He's gay, and I think he likes me."

"How do you know all this?"

"He came right out and told me he was gay. And he looked *so disappointed* when I told him about you and showed him your picture on my phone."

"I don't like this guy already."

"Now, Bradley, you've been meeting all these good-looking television stars. Surely you don't care if I met a really hot English professor," Matt teased.

"Now I *really* don't like him."

"Well, don't get too green with jealousy just yet. He hasn't been hired. Today was just an interview day for him. Besides, he would be in a different department anyway."

"Okay, but you better watch yourself if this guy gets hired. Especially after all that bizarre business with Derrick."

"I'll be careful. Anyway, I'm in love with just *you*. Remember that."

"Of course I remember. And I love just you, not these Hollywood types. But it's getting later by the minute. I guess I'd better let you get back to sleep."

"As if I could sleep now, after all your Hollywood news."

BRADLEY had barely seated himself at his desk in his office the following morning when the phone rang. He answered in a somewhat sleepy voice. "Yes?"

"There's an Alice Grant calling for you on line two, Mr. Moore."

"Thanks, Janet." Bradley punched the button on his phone. "Hello, Alice?"

"Good morning, Bradley. How are you?"

"I'm just barely here after getting up a little late. I was on the phone to Matt in New York last night, as you know, and we talked for a while. I found it hard to get to sleep with all the excitement of what we discussed at dinner about the TV show."

"That's what I called to talk to you about. What did your husband say when you told him about Cole's offer?"

"He was a little dubious about the swimming before dinner, but he got very excited about my appearing on Cole's show. He's absolutely in favor of it. What did you find out from the producer?"

"Well, there is good news and odd news."

Bradley chuckled. "What does *that* mean?"

"The producer assures me that there are indeed enough SAG members in the cast to make it acceptable for you as a non-union actor to play the part. So we're okay about that. The odd thing is that the show is going on a brief hiatus for a couple of weeks. They won't begin shooting your scene right away. Not even Cole knew this was going to happen."

"You said a couple of weeks? That sounds like the scene would be filmed during the week Matt is here."

"That's probably about right. Is that a problem?"

"Well, I don't know exactly. I'd hate for him to just sit in a hotel room for a day while I'm working on the show. My boss here at the firm is already giving me the week off to spend with him. I might not be able to be in the show after all."

"I think there's a simple enough solution, if you'd be interested. Just bring Matt along to the set and let him watch."

"Would they let us do that?"

It was Alice's turn to chuckle. "It's done all the time. Besides, if the star of the show—Cole, of course—says it's all right, then *it is all right*. I'm sure the director won't mind one extra visitor on the set. Unless Matt interferes and tries to direct the scene himself." She laughed this time.

Bradley laughed too. "I'm sure we don't have to worry about that. Matt would be excited just to be able to watch a TV show being filmed."

"Then I'll make the necessary arrangements with the studio to get him cleared with a visitor's pass, and we'll be all set. I'm excited for you, Bradley."

"Thanks, Alice. I'm excited too. And I appreciate all your help."

"It's my pleasure. Good-bye."

Bradley put down the phone. *Wow. Wait until Matt learns that he gets to be here for the big scene. That'll be something extra special for his spring break.*

Chapter SEVENTEEN

MATT was almost finished straightening up his office on the last school day before spring break when a knock on the door interrupted him.

"Yes? Come in," he called.

To Matt's surprise, David Strasser opened the door and leaned his head inside. "Hi. May I see you for a moment?"

Matt smiled. "Of course. It's really nice to see you. What brings you to our campus today?" He gestured for David to sit down.

"I just got the good news," David replied, grinning broadly. "I got the position. I'll be starting classes the first summer session in June."

"I'm so happy for you. It'll be really great to have another one of *us* on staff."

David reached up to take Matt's hand. "Here, have a seat next to me," he said, pulling Matt down beside him on the small sofa. "I got a call from the department chair yesterday to drop by today for another visit. I was so excited at what he told me just a little while ago that I wanted to share the news—so I thought of you."

"Not Kristen?"

"She's not in her office. I checked. Maybe she's already left for spring break."

"I guess you're right. Anyway, I'm very glad for you."

David scooted a little closer to Matt and took his hand. "I hope that we can become really close now that I'm part of the faculty. You and I have a lot in common, you know."

Matt withdrew his hand and turned to face David. "I'm sure that we do, but there's one thing that we don't have in common. I have a husband I love very much."

David just sat quietly and gazed at Matt.

"Don't misunderstand me, David. I like you and look forward to being friends with you. But I don't want you to think there's a chance I would cheat on Bradley and lose the love of my life. You seem like a nice guy, and I like you—but that's all there is to it. Bradley and I are legally married. We've been together for over eight years. The key word here is *together*. I have no intention of giving that up. I just wanted to be clear with you about this from the start."

David just sighed. "Okay. I get it. When I saw your wedding ring the day we met, I knew deep down that I didn't have a chance with you." He smiled. "But I just wanted to be sure. Not everyone is as devoted as you seem to be. You know what I mean. And I hope that you won't hold my feeble attempt against me."

Matt smiled back. "It's okay. I'm flattered that you liked me. And we can be friends...."

"Yeah, I know. And I look forward to meeting your... uh... Bradley, was it? Well, I guess I'd better get going. Have a great spring break in California." He rose from the sofa and shook Matt's hand.

"Thanks, David. I look forward to getting to know you this summer." He hugged him. "We don't have to be so formal. We're new friends."

MATT had deplaned from his American Airlines flight, and was strolling along the Terminal 4 walkway toward the baggage claim area. He could hardly believe he was finally here in California, almost within reach of Bradley's arms. In a surprisingly short time, Matt was wheeling his large suitcase with one arm and balancing his carry-on bag on his other shoulder while he navigated to the curbside taxi stands on the lower level outside the terminal. *Thank goodness I only packed lightweight clothes.*

He quickly found a Yellow cab and was soon on his way to the restaurant not far from the airport where he was supposed to meet Bradley. Tyler had told Bradley it might be better to meet someplace away from the airport because LAX was chaotic and difficult for first-timers to navigate *and* connect with someone at the same time. So Bradley had asked Matt to take a taxi to Truxton's Restaurant.

Matt asked for a table and was pleased to be seated not far from where Bradley sat alone at another table. He sat so he had a clear view of Bradley. They exchanged glances for a few minutes, accompanied by frequent looks at their watches as though each were waiting for someone else.

Finally, Bradley got up and walked over to Matt's table where Matt was sipping a soft drink. "Excuse me," Bradley began. "I wonder if you would mind sharing a table. I've been waiting for my boyfriend, but he hasn't shown up yet. It looked like you were waiting for someone too, so I thought we could wait together."

Matt gave him a cool stare. "That's pretty forward of you to approach a stranger like that."

"You're right. I'll go back to my table."

"No. It's okay. You can sit here. I was getting a little bored waiting by myself anyway," Matt said. He gestured to the empty chair across the table.

"Thanks. I guess I should introduce myself if we're going to sit together for a while. My name is Brad. Brad Pith."

Matt giggled. "What did you say?"

"I said Brad Pith," Brad repeated.

"Really? I thought maybe you have a lisp."

Brad glared. "I know it sounds strange, but there it is."

"Sounds a lot like the movie star Brad Pitt, you know."

"Yes, I believe that's been pointed out to me before. So, what's your name?"

"As it happens, I have a name that sounds a lot like a movie star too. It's Daniel Gregg."

"*Way to play the game, Matt*," Brad said softly, and then he grinned. "Well, you're right. That sounds a lot like Daniel Craig, the newest James Bond actor."

Daniel grinned back. "It does, doesn't it?"

"Who are you meeting here, *Daniel*?" Brad asked.

"Well, *Brad*, I'm supposed to meet my husband, the lazy bastard who's always late."

"You took the words right out of my mouth, Daniel. I have the same problem. But why do you stay with the *bastard* if he's late all the time?"

Daniel smiled gleefully. "He's pretty good in bed. He's got a really big—"

"Stop. I don't want the details. My situation, however, is a little different. My husband is only *so-so* in bed. Pretty average, actually." Brad chuckled. "Maybe even really *small*, but he does have a steady job to support me, and that's why I stay with the tardy slut."

Daniel was laughing softly. "Gee, that's a shame. But at least there's the money, though."

Brad grinned broadly. "We all have our crosses to bear, I guess."

"I have an idea," Daniel blurted. "How about we teach those two *losers* a lesson and go off together? We could go to my hotel. My husband doesn't even know where I have a reservation."

"What a good idea," Brad agreed. "You're awfully cute, much better looking than my *sorry* husband, anyway. *Let's do it.*"

"Let me just pay my check," Daniel began.

"Oh, no. That's okay. I'll take care of it, and since I just happen to have a car, we can be on our way to your hotel. I hope that it's not too far away."

THE Hollywood Roosevelt Hotel, serving visitors in style since 1927, is something of a shrine to the legend of old Hollywood. None of that mattered, however, to the two hot-for-each-other young men who eagerly rushed into their luxurious suite, slamming the door and tossing clothes aside as they leaped into bed for an afternoon of long-anticipated delights.

No longer as breathless as they had been when they had entered the suite, they awakened somewhat later after a short nap.

Matt looked sleepily over at Bradley. "What was your name again?"

"Which name do you want?" Bradley replied with a smile.

"I'll take the married name."

"I guess we can forget about Brad Pith and Daniel Gregg, then," Bradley replied.

"So true," Matt remarked. He cuddled close to Bradley. "It's so good to finally be with you again."

Bradley kissed him gently. "I know exactly what you mean. I've waited a long time for this."

"It was nice of Winston to give you a week off so we could be together," Matt said. "I like Winston."

"So do I. He's a smart man who knows how to keep his employees happy. And I'm *happy*. Of course I really work for Grace—"

"Are we going to stay in bed all afternoon or go sightseeing?" Matt interrupted.

"I'd be content to just stay in bed with my honey, but we can do that all night... and for several nights. What would you like to do? We didn't get to see very much of California on our honeymoon out here since it was such a short trip."

"Oh, I want to do all the touristy things like go to Grauman's Chinese, the Hollywood Walk of Fame, the Universal Studios tour, Knott's Berry Farm, Disneyland—"

"Whoa. All of that this afternoon?"

Matt laughed. "No, silly. That's just my tentative list. I'm sure I'll think of more later, but I'd also like to meet some of those stars you've been meeting out here."

"You're in luck, sweetheart. We're going to dinner tonight with Tyler Jensen. And since you haven't seen Elliot in a while and he already knows Tyler, I thought we'd bring Elliot too."

"That's a great idea. I can't wait."

"And I know you haven't forgotten about going with me to the studio to shoot my big scene on Cole Bristow's TV show."

"How could I ever forget that? Isn't that just a few days away?" Matt asked.

"That's right. But you're going to meet Cole and some of his friends who are stars even before that. We're invited to one of his 'swim and dine' parties at his mansion the day after tomorrow."

"I'm *so excited* about all of this," Matt said as he leaned over and gave Bradley another kiss.

"We've got a couple of hours before we have to pick up Elliot. This hotel is really close to Grauman's and the Walk of Fame. Shall we try to take in those two today?"

"Terrific," Matt agreed. "Sounds like fun."

"The only thing is, we have to watch the time a little bit. The restaurant we're going to tonight is kind of a classy place, and we have to dress for dinner. I anticipated going to places like this so that's why I warned you to bring a suit. And I hope you brought a *swimsuit* too, both for Cole's house and for the hotel pool."

"Oh, don't worry. I brought both."

"We might even brave going into the Pacific... the beach next to the Santa Monica pier, for example. The ocean's kind of *cold*, but we just *have* to go to the pier. It's so much fun."

"Back to tonight. What *is* this 'classy' place where we're going?" Matt asked.

"It's the place where Elliot and I first met Tyler. It's called Haute. We'll have to get you dressed here first, and then I'll have to dress at my apartment when we go to pick up Elliot. He bought a new car a couple of weeks ago and he can't wait to show it off to you. He convinced me that we should all three go together in the new car tonight. Be sure you *brag* about it."

"Fine. I'll do that. Maybe you should pack a few things to bring back here to the hotel. You *are* going to stay with me while I'm here, aren't you?"

Bradley grinned. "Just try to keep me away. You'll be happy to learn that I've already packed a bag. It's at the apartment ready to go. I would have brought it with me, but I was so excited to meet you at that restaurant I forgot."

"That's certainly *understandable*," Matt said, chuckling. "I don't blame you."

"Let's get going, honey. We're so close to Grauman's that we're going to walk."

"Before we go, I'd better make a confession to you," Matt said with a sigh.

"Oh? What's the confession?"

"I've been holding hands with that new English professor, David Strasser."

"What?" Bradley demanded.

"He came to my office after he got the job, and we sat on my office sofa holding hands."

"I'm going to kill this guy."

Matt looked sheepish and turned away. Then he burst out laughing. "I guess I better tell you the whole story."

When Matt finished relating the events in the office, Bradley was mollified, but only by a little. "I still don't like this guy."

"Oh, he's harmless. I think it's cute he was sort of interested in me. And to be fair, he didn't really know our background and what it means. There won't be any more *scenes* between us. I took care of that before I left."

"There better not be," Bradley said. "I'm the jealous type—even after all these years."

"Don't be so grumpy. I'm telling you there was nothing to it. Now let's forget the whole thing and head for Grauman's before it gets any later."

"YOU look very nice, Elliot," Matt declared. "I haven't seen you so dressed up in a very long time."

"Thanks, Matt. I think you're pretty too."

They both laughed.

"Okay, I'm ready at last," Bradley said as he came out of the bathroom straightening his tie. "I think I'll put my packed bags into the trunk of the rental car so I don't have to do it later this evening when we get back."

"It's already done," Matt replied. "Elliot and I took care of it while *you* were dressing and *we were waiting*." He looked at Elliot. "We were *so much younger then*...."

Elliot burst out laughing and Bradley grinned. "Ha. Ha. I didn't take *that long*."

Matt interrupted. "Shouldn't we get going?"

"You're right," Bradley agreed, and they headed for the car.

"Bradley, you sit in the back since this is Matt's first ride in my car. He can ride shotgun."

"You're dying to show off this new convertible, aren't you?"

Elliot nodded. "That's right. Now *come on.* I'll put the top down."

They quickly piled into the new blue convertible. Elliot carefully exited the apartment complex parking lot and slowly started down the street.

"You drive like my *grandmother*," Bradley griped from the back.

"Buy your *own* convertible, and let's see how you drive in this LA traffic."

"Okay, boys," Matt said. "You can fight on the playground but not in the car. Mother won't stand for it."

"Yes, *Mother*," Elliot and Bradley recited together.

After riding along for a while, Bradley spoke up. "I've got an idea."

"I don't like the sound of it already," Elliot interjected.

"Matt, how about we play a little mini-version of our game for Tyler's enjoyment?"

"Do you really know him well enough to do that with him? He's a new friend, isn't he?" Matt replied. "He might not be as amused as we are."

"We could tell him it was *Elliot's idea* and blame him if it doesn't work out," Bradley suggested.

"Thanks, guys. But I really don't know him well enough either to be playing jokes on him. What if he gets mad and walks out?" Elliot asked.

"We could tone it down a little," Bradley insisted. "But Tyler and I have become reasonably good friends. I don't think he'll mind some teasing. He's Winston's client anyway, so if anything goes wrong, it'll be my fault—not the firm's. I'll remind him of that."

"This is coming from the guy who didn't even want to play games when this all started." Matt added. "I had to practically hold a gun to his head."

"Speaking of that…," Elliot began.

"*Never mind*," Bradley and Matt chimed in together.

"We all remember the biker bar," Bradley added dryly.

"Maybe we shouldn't pull *anything* in front of him," Matt said. "I don't even know him."

"Tell you what," Bradley said as Elliot pulled into the restaurant parking lot. "We could do a little modified version, and then the whole 'game' concept will be a topic of conversation during dinner. After all, it *has* been a lot of fun—*most* of the time."

"Well, I guess we could try a few lines and see how it goes. We can stop and explain if it doesn't work out," Matt finally agreed.

"Just remember that not everyone has your *warped sense of humor*," Elliot warned.

"You go in first and get seated with Tyler. Tell him we're in the men's room or something," Bradley ordered. "We'll come in a couple of minutes later. Just follow our lead and don't tip him off before we get there."

"Okay, okay," Elliot muttered and went ahead.

After a few minutes of discussing roles and strategy, Matt and Bradley entered Haute and asked for Tyler Jensen's table.

Tyler stood and shook hands when they arrived at the table. Elliot sat in silence.

"Tyler, I'm so sorry that my husband, Matt, couldn't make the trip to LA this time. He has some sort of STD or something."

Matt glared at Bradley but said nothing.

"But the good news is that his *older* brother came instead. Tyler, meet Mitchell Sharp. He's a lot cuter than my *dreary old husband*, anyway."

Tyler had been taken aback by the STD comment, but now he merely blinked, half smiled, and shook *Mitchell's* hand. "Very nice to meet you," he muttered.

"It's nice to meet you too," Mitchell said. He turned to Bradley. "You said he was better looking on TV than in person, but I think he's really handsome."

Tyler's smile froze, Elliot ducked his head, but Bradley didn't miss a beat.

"You're being too kind, Mitchell. Besides, it was Elliot here who said he looked better on TV."

Elliot turned bright red. "That's a lie. I never... said... anything... like...," he stammered.

"Now, Bradley," Mitchell interrupted, "you were the one who said that all these Hollywood stars you've been meeting looked like plastic surgery rejects. That wasn't very nice."

Tyler's mouth had fallen open during these exchanges, and he was obviously flustered beyond words. "I just don't know what to say," he murmured.

"Well, I do," Elliot exclaimed. "This has gone *far enough*. You're not being funny at each other's expense anymore. You're being plain insulting to Tyler who doesn't have a clue what you're up to. Bradley, you explain this mess right now before I punch you in the nose."

Tyler's eyes widened.

"Oh, *all right*," Bradley agreed. "We shouldn't have taken it so far and aimed it at Tyler instead of each other. I agree that it really isn't funny anymore."

"Would someone please tell me what's going on?" Tyler asked.

"Matt started it several months ago," Bradley began.

"Don't blame it on *me*," Matt protested. "You're the one who wanted to play games for Tyler's benefit."

Tyler looked blank. "Huh?"

"Then I'll tell him," Elliot insisted. "It's a game, Tyler. Matt heard about it from a friend of ours in New York. He and Bradley started doing it to spice up their relationship. They were giving you a little sample. First of all, that's really Matt, not Mitchell. There is no Mitchell. They just made him up... along with all the other stuff."

Elliot explained the "cheating" game concept and told some of the stories that had happened during their games. The waiter interrupted at one point to take their orders, but they finally explained the game to Tyler during the meal.

"Wow," Tyler exclaimed. "That's really wild. You two ought to have your own situation comedy." He looked down at his plate. "I've hardly eaten. Your 'game' stories were really fascinating. I particularly liked the Halloween party."

Bradley blushed. "Now that wasn't really my fault."

"But it was funny anyway," Elliot jumped in. "Of course, I got the biggest charge out of the gay biker bar story since I had to rescue them from *certain death*."

"Biker bar? You didn't tell that one."

Bradley blushed a deeper red, joined by Matt this time.

"Just skip that one," Bradley insisted.

"No. Come on, Elliot, tell me about it."

Elliot seemed to relish the story more and more as he told it.

"Drugs and money in a gay biker bar?" Tyler asked, astounded.

Matt turned to Bradley. "Somebody peed his pants."

"Well, you ran screaming like a little girl down the alley," Bradley retorted.

Elliot grinned. "I think maybe this makes up a little for the mean things you two said to Tyler." He turned to Tyler. "See what I have to put up with?"

Tyler smiled. "But you love them both. Anyone can see that."

Bradley looked at Tyler. "I'm really sorry for the things we said."

"It's okay. I get it. But I'll tell you this. I haven't been so entertained at dinner in a long time."

"You were a really good sport to put up with all of this," Matt added.

"There wasn't a dull moment. That's for sure!" Tyler replied. "I know I'll never forget this evening."

"As long as you *forgive* us for it," Bradley said.

"Of course," Tyler looked at his watch. "I hate to say it, but I have an early call at the studio in the morning." He winked at Matt and then gave him a discreet kiss on the cheek. "It was lovely meeting you, and I look forward to seeing you and Bradley at Cole's dinner party." He shook hands with Elliot. "I loved your stories about the 'game'. Good night."

Chapter
EIGHTEEN

MATT and Bradley's Yellow Cab pulled away from the Hollywood Roosevelt Hotel and headed toward the studio where Bradley would have his big scene in a TV show. Despite the early hour, traffic was already heavy when the taxi forged onto the freeway.

"Are you nervous?" Matt asked.

"Not really. I don't have to do much, and it's not in front of a studio audience anyway. Thank goodness for that."

"Do you know your lines?"

"*Ha ha.* You know that I've got about three lines to say before I fall over dead on the desk," Bradley replied dryly.

"Well, that's more than most people ever get to say on a national network TV show." Matt replied. "It was very nice of Cole to do this for you."

"I know it, and I'm very grateful. By the way, how did you like Cole and his friends at that dinner party the other night?"

Matt grinned. "He's very nice, and he's just as handsome in person as I expected. His friends were nice too. Even Tyler, who seemed to really enjoy telling everyone about our little prank at the restaurant the other night."

"He *did* seem to enjoy that. Good thing for us that he's such a good sport," Bradley added.

"It still doesn't seem real that we're talking about actors that we've seen on TV as though they're our *friends*."

"They *are* becoming our friends," Bradley said, almost wistfully.

"You're going to miss them when you get back to New York, aren't you?"

"I guess. In a way, at least. But it's not like I know them all that well. We've only met a few times."

Matt was quiet for a few moments. "Do you like it out here in California?"

Bradley turned to look carefully into Matt's eyes. "I have to admit that living out here for these past few months has surprised me. I didn't expect to like it, but it's begun to grow on me. When we were out here before and got married, we didn't really get a feel for what it's like."

Matt was silent for a few moments. "Would you like to *stay* out here? Live here from now on, I mean? I could tell when we were at Disneyland and all those other tourist places that you were having a really great time."

"Not without *you*. I don't even have to think about it," Bradley replied.

"What if I could find a job at a community college or something like that? We've talked about some options that I would have out here. Would you want to live here if we could work something out?"

"Think *big*, Matt. How about USC or UCLA?" Bradley gave Matt his best smile. "But I'd like it in LA only if *you* were happy here too."

"That's sweet, Bradley. I love you for that. Well, and for *other reasons* too."

Bradley chuckled. "I certainly hope so. Anyway, this is all speculation. I haven't got a clue whether Winston would mind if I stayed out here. Not that it would matter much, I guess. Grace already told me that I could remain out here as her representative if I wanted."

"Here we are," the taxi driver announced as he looked at the meter to tell them the fare.

Bradley and Matt got out of the cab, and Bradley paid the driver. "Keep the change," he added.

"You'd better call Cole on your phone as he suggested so he can escort us to the right soundstage," Matt said. He reached into his shirt pocket for the studio passes Cole had given them the night of his party. "I'll talk to the guard at the gate and give him our passes while you call."

Moments later Cole came speeding up to the gate in a fancy golf cart with the name of the studio emblazoned all over it.

"Jump in," Cole called. "We've got to get you to makeup and wardrobe, Bradley."

In no time at all, Cole had brought them to the door of the soundstage where a man waited to take the cart away.

"Let's go inside," Cole said as he opened the door and led them through a maze of lights, cameras, wires and cables on the floor, and various crew members going about their business for the day.

As they got near the set for the day's scene, a neatly attractive and slightly older man approached. He smiled at the two men with Cole. "So this is our new talent?"

Cole laughed. "That's right. Delivered as promised, and ready for makeup. We'll put him into a nice suit too, of course. Bradley, this is our director, Steve Olsen. Steve, this is Bradley Moore."

"Glad to have you with us, Bradley," Steve said. "I hope you'll have fun doing our little scene."

"I'm sure that I will," Bradley replied, shaking Steve's hand.

"And here's the other half of this cute couple. Steve, this is Matt, or more formally, Dr. Matthew Sharp. Remember I told you that he would be on the set today too?"

"Of course." Steve smiled and shook Matt's hand too. "Any friend of Cole's is welcome to our little set."

"Thanks," Matt replied. "I've really been looking forward to this."

"Well, fellows," Cole said, "let's go through here, and I'll take Bradley to makeup. Matt, there's coffee over there so just help yourself. I'll be right back to keep you company. I don't normally report to the set for scenes I'm not in, but today is naturally an exception."

More than an hour later, Bradley found his way back to the set. This time he sported a slightly exaggerated healthy complexion and an expensive well-cut suit. Cole was waiting.

"You look terrific, Bradley. I bet you'd break a lot of ladies' hearts if you were on TV all the time."

Bradley laughed. "I'm no actor, as you're about to find out. It's a good thing I don't have to do very much."

"I'd like for you to meet someone," Cole replied. "I have a little *surprise* for you."

"Oh? What's up?" Bradley asked.

A strikingly handsome young man with wavy black hair and brilliant blue eyes walked up to the men. He smiled, and even his teeth were dazzling.

"Bradley, this is your co-star for this scene. Meet Chad Reeves, who'll be playing the part of your secretary."

Bradley blinked in surprise. "What? A *male* secretary?"

"Surprise!" Cole called out gaily. "You're going to share a passionate kiss with this lovely young man."

"But I thought the secretary was a *girl*," Bradley stumbled.

"I was afraid you wouldn't want to play the part if you knew otherwise. Is there a problem?"

Bradley licked his lips. "Not exactly, but does Matt know about this?"

"Oh yes. I told him while you were in makeup. He didn't seem to mind a bit."

"Well, I guess it's all right, then. No offense, Chad. I just was a little surprised. That's all."

Chad laughed and shook Bradley's hand. "It's okay. I'm just glad I get to kiss someone really *cute like you*."

"Don't you two enjoy yourselves *too much*," Cole warned. "Bradley, this is my new boyfriend, so don't get carried away." He laughed as the other two grinned.

Steve walked onto the set at that point. "If you two gentlemen are ready, let's do a quick rehearsal. Our stand-in actors have already helped set the lighting so I think we're ready for a trial run. By the way, gentlemen, since you are both new to this, I'll tell you that we only do one or two takes. This isn't the movies where they might do twenty-five or more takes. We simply don't have the budget for that. Let's get it done right the first, or maybe second, time. Places, please. Bradley, right over here at this desk. Chad, you stand over there and get ready to make your entrance."

"Where's Matt?" Bradley whispered to Cole. "He'll miss everything."

"Don't worry," Cole replied. "He's in the restroom or something. He won't mind missing this first part. It's just a rehearsal."

"Ready, Bradley?" Steve asked. At a nod from him, Steve called out, "Action!"

Bradley sat at the desk, pretending to work on some papers. From offstage Chad said his line, and Bradley replied. Chad entered the office, said his line, and waited. Bradley said a line, and they kissed. Bradley said his last line, and Chad left the office. Bradley sat down and appeared to be clearing his desk when a man in black approached. Bradley looked up, and the man held out a gun, paused, and fired a blank shot. Bradley looked stunned and fell forward.

"Great," roared Steve from the sidelines. "That's just perfect. Almost. Bradley, you're not kissing your *grandmother*. Give it a little more passion, please. Now we'll do it for the cameras. Bradley, let me tell you, since this is your first time. Keep going through the scene no matter what happens. Stay in character and say your lines, just as we rehearsed. Don't let the added lighting or cameras or anything else throw you. Okay?"

Bradley looked a little puzzled, but he nodded. He didn't have time to look for Matt.

"Lights! Cameras! Action!" Steve bellowed.

The scene progressed just as it had in rehearsal. The men said their lines, kissed, and Bradley sat down again at the desk. Then things suddenly changed.

Matt charged onto the set while a stunned Bradley looked at him in disbelief.

"What are *you* doing here?" Bradley gasped.

"I came to see for myself what a two-timing *cheat* you really are," Matt yelled. He slapped Bradley and stormed out of the office.

Then the man in black slowly entered, held up his gun, and shot Bradley who fell forward, still in a state of shock.

"*Wonderful!*" called Steve. "That was just *beautiful*. There was just the right look of shock on Bradley's face before he died."

Bradley sat up. "*What's going on here?*" he demanded.

Matt walked back to the desk. "Surprise," he sang out.

Cole was laughing, almost doubled over, as he joined Matt and Bradley on the set. "I'm sorry, Bradley, but we rewrote the scene just a little bit when we learned that Matt would be here. We thought it would add some extra drama, even though the male secretary will be something of a surprise for the audience too."

Steve now joined them on the set. "I apologize for keeping the changes from you, Bradley. But as a non-professional, you might not have shown the reactions I wanted if you knew that Matt would be in the scene too. We had to hurry him into makeup while you were in a different makeup room."

Bradley glared at Matt. "You *knew* about all this, of course."

Sheepishly, Matt nodded. "They sent me a script a couple of days ago. I had to hide it from you to keep up the surprise. I'm sorry if I scared you, sweetie."

Bradley sat still for moment, thinking it over. At last he smiled. "Okay. I get it. It really works for the scene, I guess. I just couldn't believe it when you charged over to me and slapped me. That was a pretty hard slap too, Matt."

"We *actors* try to do our best." Matt replied, chuckling. "I hope I didn't really hurt you though."

"Not really. But this has been much more of an *experience* than I ever thought it would be."

Matt grinned. "Just playing the game, Bradley. Just playing the game."

Steve interrupted. "Now that the fun is over, we need to get a few close-ups before we're finished. We need a shot of the gun, and we need a close shot of Bradley dead on the desk. Stay still while we apply some stage blood. Ready?"

Bradley obediently laid his head on the desk after the blood was applied, and the close-ups began.

Chapter
NINETEEN

MATT sat nervously in the living room of his New York apartment. Bradley was due any minute from the airport. Flights still made Matt worry, even though he knew the statistics were in favor of Bradley's safe arrival home.

Over four months. That's how long Bradley has been gone. It seems like a year. It even seems like a year since I was with Bradley in California for spring break, and that was really only about six weeks ago. But at last Bradley's coming home for good.

Matt's heart jumped a beat when he heard the key in the lock of their front door. Bradley opened the door and grinned broadly as he hurried inside. Matt flew into his arms, and they shared a lengthy kiss.

"Oh, sweetheart," Matt murmured. "I thought you'd never get here."

"There were a few hitches at the airport, but I'm here now."

Matt stepped back to look at Bradley and suddenly his smile faded. "You're only carrying your carry-on bag. You don't have your *suitcases*."

"Oh, that," Bradley began.

"You've decided to stay in California, haven't you?" Matt gasped. "That's why you only have the one bag. I *knew* this was going to happen. I could tell when I was out there in California. You've decided to live out there, haven't you?"

"Now wait a minute, Matt."

Matt burst into tears. "I'll try to be a good sport about this," he sobbed. "I liked California too, but I didn't really expect you to *move out there*."

"Give me a chance to explain, honey."

Matt tried to dry his tears with his shirt sleeve. "No. It's okay, Bradley. I'll try to find a job out there someplace, even if I have to flip burgers at McDonald's! I'll go and try to make the best of it somehow. 'Would you like fries with that?' I'm just practicing."

"Matt, sweetie, just *shut up*," he thundered. "You haven't given me a chance to say anything. The airline lost my luggage. That's all there is to it. I'm not moving to LA."

At last Matt was stunned into silence. "Oh," was all he could manage.

Bradley grinned and put his arms around Matt again. "Did you really think I'd make a decision that big without talking to you first? You shock me, sweetheart."

Matt sniffed and said, "Well, I thought it was kind of an ugly surprise for you to do something like that. But now I think about it, I see how silly I was. I'm sorry, Bradley."

"Forget it, Matt. We're back together, and that's that. Do you have any real coffee? That stuff on the plane isn't all that good."

A FEW hours later, Bradley and Matt sat together on the living room sofa, cuddled up and cozy.

"That was a splendid homecoming," Bradley said with a smirk, glancing toward the bedroom.

"We're not so out of practice, despite our time apart," Matt added with a wink.

"Let's not ever get out of practice."

"Agreed."

"You know, Matt, I really did have a good time in California."

Matt nodded. "I know you did."

"And I actually thought about talking to both Winston and Grace about staying out there—with you joining me, of course."

"I figured as much," Matt replied.

"But then I got to thinking about New York. We have a wonderful life here. We're already settled into our little place. You've got a great job, and so do I. LA is very exciting, and I loved it. But it's just *not home*. You and I are the real thing—real New Yorkers."

"That's right, Bradley. We are."

"And now that we have friends out West—Elliot and Tyler and Cole and all the others—we have somebody to go visit whenever we want."

"Yes," Matt agreed, "and those same friends can come to New York whenever they like. We can show them around and share all that New York has to offer. Who knows? Some of our actor friends might even want to try Broadway or maybe television out here."

"True," Bradley said. "And there's something else."

"What's that?"

"Besides all that we have in New York, there's something else too. We have each other and lots more 'cheating games' to be played in the city."

Matt laughed and nodded.

A knock sounded on the front door.

"I wonder who that can be," Bradley asked with a grin.

"You can probably guess," Matt replied, and he strolled to the door to let Clarice enter.

She rushed into the room and grabbed for Bradley, almost before he had a chance to stand up. "You're back. Bratt is back together," she gushed.

"Oh, *brother*," Bradley said with a smile. "I'd forgotten all about that name."

"Well, I didn't," Clarice said. "I've missed seeing the two of you."

Another knock sounded on the front door.

"Who else did you invite, Matt? It couldn't be Elliot since he's still in LA."

Matt opened the door to a man in uniform with three very large suitcases. "Mr. Bradley Moore?" he asked.

"Over there," Matt replied, pointing to Bradley who was already reaching for his wallet to give the man a tip.

"Thanks," the uniformed man said with a smile as he looked at the size of the tip. "Thanks a lot."

"Now things are *nearly* back to normal," Bradley said.

"At least until we figure out another *cheating game*," Matt replied.

EPILOGUE

"KRISTEN, would you please take that bowl of popcorn into the living room? And Clarice, I'd appreciate it if you'd help me with these drinks."

"Sure, Matt," Kristen replied. She also grabbed a stack of paper cups to be used with the popcorn and then she headed to the other room.

"There are only four of us, Matt," Clarice said. "You want to bring those two, and I'll take the others?"

"Sure. Thanks for the help," Matt said as he picked up the drinks. "Where's Bradley?"

"He's out in the living room waiting for his *big moment*," Clarice said with a grin. "He's going to be *insufferable* after this, I'm afraid."

"He'll get over it, Clarice. The whole scene only lasts a couple of minutes."

"Everybody take a seat," Bradley exclaimed. "The network previews are on now so the show starts in just a few seconds."

They all sat together on the sofa, eyes glued to the television screen.

Sure enough, there was the sign on the office door, identifying the setting. The camera panned across the darkly lit office and stopped on Bradley, lighted by a desk lamp, working hard at his desk. The buzzer sounded, the secretary spoke, and the surprise of there being a male secretary registered on Clarice's and Kristen's faces. The handsome secretary entered, spoke, and kissed Bradley.

The little home audience, including Matt and Bradley, said, "Ooooooh."

After the secretary left, Matt stormed into the scene, hollered at Bradley, and the smack of the slap sent even Bradley back in his seat on the sofa. The shock on Kristen's and Clarice's faces was palpable.

The gunman entered, drew a gun, fired at Bradley, and Bradley fell dead in a pool of blood.

The credits for *Danger Drives Me* began, and Matt pushed the mute button.

The little audience cheered and clapped in thunderous applause.

"But don't we get to see the rest of it?" Clarice complained.

"I'm recording it for later. I thought you'd like to talk about the beginning scene," Matt said.

Kristen turned to Matt. "You didn't tell me that there was a *male secretary*, and you certainly never said that *you* were in the scene too."

"Bradley and I thought that we'd save all the surprises for the broadcast. So what did you think of our little epic?"

"I think you were both terrific," Kristen replied. "And wait until your students show up in class next time. Then you'll get some *real reviews*. I'm sure they'll all think the scene was *wonderful*."

"I hope the dean of our department agrees. I didn't warn him about my being on the show."

"Honey," Clarice said to Bradley, "I can't believe your luck. You've already got cute little Matt, but then in the show you got the chance to kiss that doll face of a secretary too."

Bradley would have loved to tell them all that Chad was Cole's new boyfriend, but he kept his lips sealed. But he gave Matt a knowing look that Matt returned with a smile.

"I guess you'll both be moving to Hollywood to continue your careers in television," Kristin said with a wink.

"We talked about it," Bradley confirmed, "but we decided that you two couldn't get along without us. We're going to make the supreme sacrifice and stay in New York."

"Oh *gag*," Clarice retorted. "Be still, my heart."

"How about we just watch the rest of the show?" Matt replied. "I can run the recording back to the beginning, and we'll find out who killed Bradley and why."

"Great idea. Bradley's murder is my favorite part of the show so far, though," Clarice said.

Bradley pulled Matt over onto his lap and began kissing him. Between kisses he said, "It's lucky that the whole thing is just like a *game*."

GENE TAYLOR was born about fifty miles south of Dallas in Corsicana, Texas, and he actually got to see what the city looked like twenty-six years later when he visited it briefly for the first time. He grew up in a different part of the state and thus knew very little about his birthplace. He had heard that there was a bakery there that sold wonderful fruit cakes for Christmas presents, however!

He graduated from a large university in Texas with a double major in English and history, a few years later earning a master's degree at the same school. Since then he has lived in California, Arizona, Illinois, and Texas while teaching high school and selling antiques and collectibles in various shops. Currently, he has a booth in an antiques mall, but he usually spends his time writing novels and short stories. In addition, he often allots some time to play records on his restored 1947 Rock-Ola jukebox and his 1961 Wurlitzer 2500 jukebox!

At the moment he is single, but he never gives up hope of finding someone to share his interests in reading, writing, antiquing, and playing slot machines and roulette in Las Vegas! You can write to him at genetaylor957@yahoo.com.

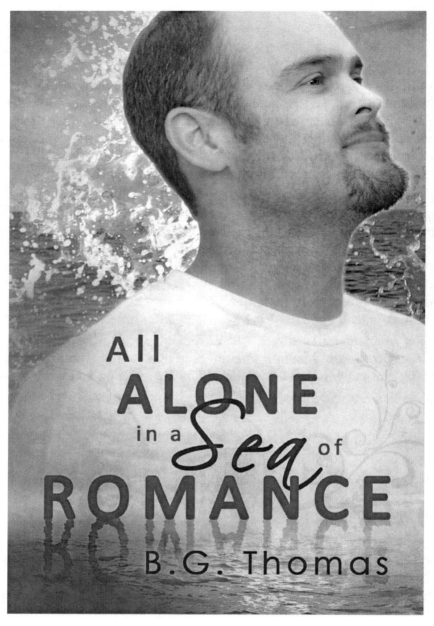

SHY

John
Inman

CPSIA information can be obtained at www.ICGtesting.com
Printed in the USA
LVOW120722110113

315136LV00001B/39/P